Also by Julia Osborne

Falling Glass
The Midnight Pianist (Book 1 in the series)

Short stories published in various magazines,
literary journals and anthologies,
broadcast on ABC Radio National,
and adaptations for stage performance

www.juliamaryosborne.com

PLAYing WiTH Keys

Julia Osborne

ETT Imprint
IN ASSOCIATION WITH
PAPER HORSE DESIGN & PUBLISHING
2016

2016 ETT Imprint Paperback Edition
in association with Paper Horse Design & Publishing

National Library of Australia Cataloguing-in-Publication entry:
Osborne, Julia, author
Playing with keys / by Julia Osborne.
ISBN 9781925416619 (pbk.)
9781925416602 (ebk.)
Romance fiction,
Pianists—Fiction
A823.4

Set in Adobe Garamond Pro 11.5/15pt by Rosie Sutherland for Paper Horse
Titles: Wednesday Sutherland — Musical motifs: Julia Osborne
www.paperhorsedesign.com.au

Life seems to go on without effort
when I am filled with music

– George Eliot, *The Mill on the Floss* (1860)

One.

On the first morning that she woke up in her family's new home, Sandra looked out the bedroom window but all she could see was the neighbour's brick wall. She sat on the side of her bed to think about it…

In Curradeen, her upstairs bedroom window in the bank residence overlooked the main street, where on countless Saturday mornings she'd watched through her curtains for Nick Morgan to drive into town, park his dusty ute across the road, and stroll into the newsagency.

All gone now. Gone, Nick and the polocrosse ponies. Gone, her dear piano teacher, the familiar high school, bicycle rides to the creek. And gone, best friend Emilia, consigned to a papery chaff of letters.

Her parents were happy with the move; she could see it in their faces. It was a good promotion for Don to the Randwick branch of the bank, and Angela was pleased to be back in Sydney after so many years in a country town. While her younger sister Prue danced around with excitement, it was only Sandra who rebelled.

Stupid brick wall. Prue's bedroom had the same dull view, but she'd shrugged and said she didn't care. Still, Sandra had to agree it was a very nice house that her father had bought, in a quiet street lined with similar old houses: tiled front veranda, hallway down the middle, and a garden out the back. After pouring over glossy catalogues with Prue, it had been fun choosing their furniture in a city department store, and Sandra was happy with her brand new bedroom suite...

Searching for a handkerchief in her dressing table, she found the Violet Crumble wrapper – souvenir of the rainy winter evening when she'd bumped into Nick at the Silver Moon Café. Back then, she hardly knew him – a hello at the polocrosse, a brief barn dance at Denalbo hall... little more.

She smoothed the wrapper with a fingernail, remembering how Nick had smiled in recognition, raised a quizzical eyebrow at her damp hair, the briefcase clutched to her chest.

Thrilled by this unexpected encounter, words had tumbled from her mouth: 'I've been to a piano lesson, my sixth grade exam's next week...' She stopped, suddenly tongue-tied.

'Wow, maybe one day you'll be a famous pianist,' he'd answered, his eyes dark under the café lights, glisten of rain on his hair.

'I'd love to try...' she'd managed to say.

Then Nick had shouted Sandra the Violet Crumble bar, and told her he'd won at poker. She remembered her shiver of excitement. Nick was a gambler! But he'd gambled with his life, that October night when he stepped into his ute with Angus.

Tired of unpacking, Sandra shoved the cardboard boxes of winter clothes under her bed. In two weeks it would be Christmas, and weeks of summer holidays stretched vacantly ahead of her – no friends, no plans, nowhere to go except the beach. The comfort of Curradeen was so far, far away, lodged in memory. Tearing a sheet of paper from her mother's writing pad, she scrabbled around to find a biro.

23 Tyrell St,
Randwick, N.S.W.,
Friday, 9th December, 1960.

Dearest Emilia,

We've been here one whole week. It was horrible when we said goodbye at the train but I tried not to cry. Did you cry too? I waved till I couldn't see you anymore and Mum wouldn't stop talking about how good it's going to be.

We put butter on Ginger's paws so he would be too busy licking it off to run away. One morning he brought home a rat and it was still half alive and Dad had to hit it with a hammer. I thought I'd be sick.

Our house is nice, it's very old but it's all fixed up. I liked my old bedroom better. We don't have bank furniture anymore so Mum bought lots of new things. I've got a beautiful Queen Anne bed and a dressing table with fancy mirrors. It feels odd having real neighbours and not another bank. My bedroom faces the brick wall next door, Prue's room is on the wall side too but she couldn't care less. Mum and Dad have a nicer bedroom, they can see the garden.

I skipped the last few days of school but we went to see the headmistress and I can start next year. She's short as me and ties her hair in a little bun. I won't miss Wilkins or Crow but Miss Pearce was nice for English and I hope I have a teacher like her.

Remember our pact to be friends forever? I miss you so much, please write really really soon and pleeease tell me if you ever see Nick.

Love forever,
Sandra xoxoxox

What would Nick be doing right now? The last she'd seen of him after the accident, he'd been lying asleep in a hospital bed.

Oh, that awful morning – believing Nick had been killed when his ute crashed, she'd run away to grieve alone in the bush. But it wasn't Nick at the wheel that moonlit night – it was Angus who crashed, swerving to miss a black swan on the road, invisible until the last moment. Now Angus was dead, and Nick had to learn to walk again.

Mrs Morgan hadn't told her much, except that because her son was a strong boy, he'd soon be back helping his father run their merino stud on Wilga Park. Mrs Morgan said we should pray for his recovery. Pray, for heavens sake! What good would that do?

Sandra wondered if she should send him a get well card. But what could she write? It was three months since the crash on Denalbo Road, and if she was going to send a card it should've been back then. Three months since she'd sneaked out of home in the middle of the night, crept into the dimly lit ward, sat by Nick's bed, watched over his quiet breathing, his bruised face.

Dear Nick, this is just to say, hurry up and get better and I hope you will soon be playing polocrosse again… no, that was awful. *Dear Nick, best wishes from all our family for a speedy recovery…*

What she really wanted to say was: *Dear Nick, I miss you terribly, I know I wasn't your girlfriend, but we had such a good time the day we met in Sydney last September holidays, and you said I looked like the girl in the painting and bought me a pie in the Rowe Street tea room. I wish I could see you again, and dance with you again, and I hope you can ride Toffee again soon…*

Oh Nick, I miss you. All those Saturday mornings I waited for you at my window, longing to speak to you, and you had no idea.

She regarded her reflection in the mirror. The same old face stared back. Same long, fair hair and urky brown eyes, same skinny self, not even a little bit taller. Turning side-on, she surveyed her profile, but the small rise of her bust remained the same small rise.

You would think, she reasoned, that after all I've been through I might look a bit different, sort of more grown up. Oh well, I'll be fifteen in April, there's still hope!

¶

Aunt Meredith was magnificent the day the Abbotts arrived in Sydney. Sleek in black Capri pants, crisp blouse and a skitter of high heels, red hair flying, she whirled into their new home with an armful of yellow roses, her wrists a jangle of bangles amidst the boxes of china and saucepans surrounding Angela in the kitchen.

'Dinner at my place,' she insisted. 'I'll drive over and get you at six sharp.' And, heels clicking, she skittered out the gate, Angela giving a sigh of relief as she gathered up towers of discarded newspaper. 'If only Meredith would just quieten down a little. Your father will get here tomorrow with the cat. We can manage.'

'We can't,' Sandra objected. 'We haven't unpacked half our things yet. I want to go.'

Thank goodness for auntie!

At dinner, as Meredith poured a glass of wine for Angela and herself to toast a welcome, she summed it up in a few words: 'Life is full of variables. All our paths – both real and imaginary – criss-cross down different roads.' She sipped her wine, with a knowing smile. 'Make of it what you will.'

To a background of piano music, seated under the climbing roses in her courtyard garden, Meredith served *quiche au fromage* with salad in painted Spanish bowls, and the promise of cassata for dessert.

Starving, Sandra immediately sliced her tart. Prue always ate like a pig, she thought, watching her sister across the table. She envied Prue's ability to slide unruffled into any situation – there seemed nothing that she regretted. Sandra glanced at her mother, fussily picking at odd bits of salad on her plate.

'Artichoke hearts,' Meredith enlightened her. 'I cooked them myself… from the thistle family,' she added, over Prue's smothered laughter.

Unconvinced, Angela pushed the odd little vegetables to one side of her plate. There was something about her sister-in-law that she couldn't understand. 'Flighty,' she'd once told Don. 'Generous, but flighty.'

No matter how Angela phrased it, commenting: 'Meredith lives very comfortably, but she hasn't a job, so how on earth does she manage?' Don brushed the question away. Or Angela would hint, 'She's never married, I can't imagine how she provides for herself.' With a shrug of his shoulders, 'Meredith has always had private means,' was all Don offered. 'She did some dressmaking when she was younger, but our father didn't believe in women working.' So that was the end of it. Meredith kept her secret.

Sandra probed her salad for the tiny sweet tomatoes, still pondering Aunt Meredith's earlier remark about how all our paths criss-cross… What paths, real or imaginary?

She would think about it later in bed.

15 Bentley St.,
Curradeen, N.S.W.,
17th December, 1960.

Dear Sandy,

Thank you for your letter. I hope you are well. I miss you too, its not the same now your gone. School has broke up and I have to work in the shop like always. Lucky you to miss some school, nothing happens at the end of term, its all muck up days.

My Nonna (mamma's mother) is coming to live with us because my grandpa is gone all strange and dont know who she is so his in hospital. I rode my bike to the cemetry on Sunday like we use to. There were people there so I didnt stay and I didnt see Angus's grave.

I never saw Nick yet but I will tell you if I see him. The new people in your old bank have a little kid. It's nearly Christmas and I wish you still lived here. I'm sorry I dont write real good letters in English, I never wrote one before.

Love from
Emilia xxx
P.S. Yes I remember our pact XOX

1

Once upon a magical time the Abbots lived a half hour drive to the Denalbo polocrosse field. Now they lived a ten minute drive to the beach. Strange to live so near the sea.

Oh, it was fun for their annual family holiday at Aunt Meredith's home in Bronte: packed into the car with beach towels, buckets and bathing caps, to drive to Bondi or Bronte beach every day, becoming salty-skinned and brown as toast, noses plastered with zinc cream. Best of all, on a low tide in the early morning, Sandra loved to search for pearly jingle shells on the smooth, washed-clean sand.

Although she ventured into the surf readily enough, trailing after her father, she never lost her fear of sharks. She hated the shriek of the siren when lifesavers spotted a dark shape cruising in the swell, the mad rush of swimmers to get out of the water. The thought of tiger sharks kept her close to the shore, itchy with sand in her bathers, picking at the sunburned flaking skin on her arms and legs, ignoring Prue's shrill insult, Sooky baby!

Encouraged by the beckoning arms of her parents, Sandra would gather her courage and – dodging between the colourful umbrellas and sunbakers sprawled glistening with coconut oil – return to the hushing, lapping waves.

It was always the same. Maybe one day she would get used to the beach – give up comparing it with the essential freedom of the bush.

Sandra's memory of an earlier home was hazy. It was as if she'd always lived in the small town surrounded by bushland and farms, being part of the small town bustle, and getting home early from school with time to do whatever she liked before piano practice.

Long ago she had promised herself to strive for the day when rainbow-coloured ribbons of music sang from her fingertips as easily as the songs she made up: to be the best possible pianist, invited to play in recitals and concerts all over the country – all over the world! She'd excelled in the concert last August, and everyone said her *Clair de Lune* was beautiful and by far the best performance of the evening. Her elderly teacher, Miss Brooks, resplendent in black with a crystal choker, her white hair rinsed blue, had almost cried.

Sure, when she left school, she'd want to go to university and study at the Sydney Conservatorium of Music – but not yet, not yet! She was just getting to know Nick, they'd even had that one perfect day in Sydney when Nick's father sent him to enquire about the School of Agriculture at university, and she had cleverly wangled a visit for the same dates, to stay with Aunt Meredith. She and Auntie had visited the Conservatorium – Sandra's excuse to her parents – while seeing Nick was a secret.

Together Sandra and Nick had explored Rowe Street, the inner city narrow lane lined with enticing little shops and arty studios that Aunt Meredith called a *bohemian cosmopolis*. Best of all, they'd visited the Art Gallery … and while wandering the halls, Nick told her she looked like the girl in the painting, and when they said goodbye, he had kissed her on the forehead.

It had been so wonderful – she was sure it was the beginning of something special – until Nick's accident drew a curtain across her happiness, and her family packed up and moved to Randwick.

Flung there, ready or not, she was faced with a new school, no friends, and surrounded by her family who were all so annoyingly happy.

23 Tyrell St,
Randwick, N.S.W.,
6th January, 1961.

Dearest Emmy,

Happy New Year! I got your letter on New Year's Eve. Did your family have a party? We don't know anyone so we stayed home and watched TV till midnight. Mum and Dad sang Auld Lang Syne and it was so sad when they sang Should old acquaintance be forgot that I cried in bed. I didn't want to make a New Year's resolution because what for? I would only want to go back to Curradeen and that's not going to happen.

Don't worry if your English isn't perfect, neither is mine. You're lucky to have your granny live with you. I never knew my grandparents, I was too little when they got old and died.

Sometimes when I wake up in the morning I forget I'm here and I think what will we do today, you and me, and all of a sudden I remember that I don't live there anymore and we've had Christmas in Sydney and Aunt Meredith cooked a big turkey dinner. We never had turkey at home. That's funny, I just wrote at home without thinking, because this is home now.

I still haven't seen our neighbours but sometimes we hear them in the back yard. I don't think they have any children unless they've left home. I liked it better when I knew people in the street and they said hello. We get our milk delivered in bottles now instead of a billycan on the front step from the dairy.

Are you working in the shop the whole holidays? Remember all those jelly babies we ate, I bet you pinched them. No, not really.

I'm sorry I didn't write much before but we spent the whole time unpacking and then it was Christmas. We all got beach towels for presents and on Sunday we're going to Bondi. We have been here exactly 36 days not counting the day we arrived.

Love from your best friend,
Sandra xoxoxo

15 Bentley St.,
Curradeen, N.S.W.,
6th January, 1961.

Dear Sandy,

It feels ages since you left. We had a big Christmas like always. I got a brush and comb set and a necklace of china beads. We went to midnight Mass and Mamma cooked roast duck and afters was Nonna's special "picciddati ring cake" which takes ages to make, a pastry ring filled with armands, figs and wallnuts and lots of honey and I ate too much and slept all afternoon.

Mrs Morgan came in the shop yesterday but Mum served her and I didn't get to ask about Nick. She bought some vegies and went out.

I saw Lofty down the street, he still makes silly faces like at school. I don't have any more news.

Love from Emmy xxx

15 Bentley St.,
Curradeen, N.S.W.,
Australia Day, 26th January, 1961.

Dear Sandy,

I got your letter and it's funny we both wrote the same day. I've never been to the beach.

Pa says Joan Sutherland is Australian of the Year. I bet she lives in Sydney. Do you know her? You'll know everyone now you live there.

You can get The Pill in Australia now but you got to be married and maybe you would have to make a confession to the priest. In maths class a girl got caught passing "Peyton Place" round under the desks and got into big trouble, they said it's real dirty.

Its 104 today and Pa's tomatoes got sunburned.

I use to pinch the jelly babies. Don't forget me your friend.

Love from Emmy XXX

1

On their first day at Randwick Girls High School, Prue pulled tight the belt on her blue and white striped cotton dress, happily putting on her new straw hat, whereas Sandra complained to her reflection, 'Look at me, I'm dressed like a juvenile.'

Prue disappeared immediately after assembly to the first year classroom, while Sandra, lost for direction, wandered up and down the stairs with nobody to tell her where to go until she found a prefect, who then sent her to the wrong room. Humiliating!

When she reached her third year classroom, the teacher had begun to call the roll and was querulously asking, 'Sandra Abbott, please. Where is Sandra Abbot?' More humiliation as a titter of laughter ran around the room, and speared by dozens of curious eyes, she found a spare desk.

23 Tyrell St,
Randwick, N.S.W.
10th February, '61.

Dearest Emmy,

I'd rather forget my first day at school it was so horrible. I didn't know where to find my classroom and walked around like an idiot for ages, everyone staring because I'm new. The school's a big, old 2 storey brick building and I still sometimes get lost.

I haven't any friends here and mostly all they talk about is going to the beach. I wanted to sit by myself but the teacher made a girl called Carol sit with me. She has frizzy hair and freckles, poor thing. She told me I'm stuck up but I don't think I am.

Dad drives us to school on his way to work but when we get used to it we'll get the bus. Prue is in class 1A. There is nowhere nice to ride our bikes. Do you ever go to the roller skating rink? I miss being able to go to your place after school. "Peyton Place" must be very rude to be banned, did you get to read any?

Mum found me a piano teacher. He lives in a flat a few blocks from our place and his name is Mr. L'estrange, I think he made it up. My first lesson is next Tuesday. I wish I still had Miss Brooks, even though she was old. Mum says I'll get used to it.

Love from Sandra xoxox

two.

The headmistress had recommended Eric L'estrange to teach Sandra seventh grade piano until she auditioned for the Conservatorium High School later that year.

'In case you're wondering,' she had explained to Angela in the principal's office, 'L'estrange is a very old English name. He's certainly not your usual type of teacher but he's highly skilled and has top qualifications from England.'

Angela was delighted. Qualifications from England! And Sandra could simply walk to his flat for her weekly lesson.

Sandra gazed at the gold letters set above the keyboard: *Feurich*, a smaller *Leipzig*. Her own Beale looked very plain compared with this tall, gleaming piano with the strange name, and straight away she wanted to run her fingers over the ivories. She waited for her new teacher to speak.

'According to your mother,' Mister L'estrange remarked, 'you aspire to being a classical concert pianist. Hmm, we shall see. Your mother also said that you started tuition when you were nine...' Sandra heard him click his tongue. 'Nine years old is quite late to begin lessons.'

Hoping to impress him, she said, 'When I was nine, we went the Town Hall. My mother got tickets for a famous pianist – that's what made me want to learn piano—'

'Who played, do you remember?'

Sandra desperately racked her brain but no name surfaced. 'Oh gosh, I can't think … I remember he played Chopin—'

'But you don't remember his famous name, hmm?' Mister L'estrange looked quizzically at her as he sorted sheet music from his files.

Embarrassed and angry, Sandra wished she could slide under the piano and disappear. Should she look at the keyboard or the teacher? She looked down at her hands, fingernails perfectly cut and buffed to a gleam. He flicked a strand of black hair from his eyebrow, spun on his heel to regard her – as if, she thought, I'm an insect under a microscope.

Closing the files, he placed the score for Elgar's *Dream Children* on the piano, 'Sight-reading,' he announced. 'You may read this briefly, then play the piece.'

It didn't look too difficult, but maybe there was a trick? Still smarting at his rebuke, she followed Miss Brook's advice: take a deep breath, count to three. The keys were silky under her fingers, the tone beautiful, and she thought she played the piece quite well as the notes went dancing sweetly across the page …

Abruptly, Mister L'estrange motioned her to stop. 'Not bad,' he commented, without smiling. 'If you could not play it properly, I didn't wish to teach you.' Again he flicked his dark hair.

How dare he say 'Not bad' as if she was barely good enough to sit at his precious piano. Sandra felt herself rebel, and bit her lip so as to remain silent. Now she was stuck with this horrid teacher. Mister L'estrange – what sort of a stupid name was that!

She looked up into the darkest brown eyes she'd ever seen, the glint of earring in his black hair. He smiled – a brilliant smile that showed neat white teeth.

How could her mother like this awful man? She would complain tonight, as soon as she got home. He was a foreigner!

23 Tyrell St, Randwick, N.S.W.,
Tuesday, 21st February, '61.

Dear Emmy,

At my first piano lesson Mr. L'estrange was so nasty. He made me do a test and he was really rude but Mum didn't want to talk about it. She thinks he's the ants pants. He calls me Sarn-dra and he has long hair!

Today's lesson was better. He told me Percy Grainger died yesterday and he played "Country Gardens" as a memorial song. He plays really well so maybe he's all right for a teacher. He said he used to play piano at home in his pyjamas that his mother sewed for him. I mean Percy Grainger not Mr. L'estrange.

Have you seen Mrs Morgan again or Nick or anyone apart from Lofty? Tell me some exciting NEWS!

Aunt Meredith said one day we'll go into town to the shops and have lunch at Mark Foys or David Jones, just the two of us. I'd rather go to DJs and see their piano player. He wears a tuxedo and plays a shiny, black grand piano and I like how he looks all around while he plays.

We're reading "The Merchant of Venice" and "The History of Mr. Polly" by H.G. Wells, which I like because it's funny and old-fashioned. We did a poem by Elizabeth Riddell about a lifesaver that drowned. I like it better than lots of English poems. The lady teachers for English and Geography are very nice thank goodness. I'm glad I don't do French as the other kids don't like the teacher.

Carol asked me to go to the beach with her but I didn't want to because my swimming costume is all wrong and I always get dumped by a wave.

It's been raining and today was boiling hot.

Love from Sandra xxx

P.S. Mr. L'estrange has an earring!! I bet he didn't wear it when he met Mum.

15 Bentley St.,
Curradeen, N.S.W.,
Friday, 3rd March, 1961.

Dear Sandy,

I got your letter and I think maybe its nice to go to a big school and not sit in stinky hot classrooms like ours. Tony left school after his Intermediate and works at the flour mill. Boo hoo. Anyway I don't mind, he never would have liked me.

Guess what, Lofty asked me to go with him !! We have "Henry V" for Shakespeere and our book is "The Passage" which is about fishing in the ocean. That story "The Monkey's Paw" gave me a nightmare. I didn't get to read the rude book.

There was a grass fire between here and Denalbo but they put it out real quick and no sheep got burnt. Pa says there are big bushfires in Western Australia from lightening, and nearly a million acres got burned and some buildings. I'd be so scared.

I have to work at the shop after school every day. I haven't seen Mrs Morgan again. Your piano teacher sounds scary. Whose Percy Granger?

Love from Emmy xxxOOO

23 Tyrell St,
Randwick.

10 / 3 / 61.

Dear Emmy,

Are you really going with Lofty? We called him googly eyes because he was an annoying little squirt, so why? He's all right, I suppose. It's better with no boys at school. Remember how Wilkins raved on to the boys in Geography about his old university days and what a good time he had? I hated him. I don't like the Merchant of Venice, it's horrible, about asking for a pound of flesh to pay a debt. I don't know how it ends yet.

Mum and Dad like living here. It's a long walk to the shops but I'm getting used to it. Prue sometimes comes with

16

me. She's made lots of friends already, lucky thing. She came a cropper off her bike and got into trouble for riding on a main road.

Mr. L'estrange doesn't look old for a music teacher. I think he might be a gypsy, his hair is very inky black. In my last lesson, the phone rang while I was playing and I tried to play with long pauses but I couldn't hear what he said except it wasn't English. He's got the blackest eyes I've ever seen.

I can't believe Tony would leave school, what a drip. Sorry, but he is, I never knew why you had such a crush.

On Saturday I'm going by myself to the Art Gallery specially to see a painting I like.

I've got to practice before dinner, I'll write more next time. Percy Grainger was a world famous pianist.

Love from Sandra XXOO

9

Today was the day. If she couldn't go with Nick, she would go by herself. From the front steps of the Art Gallery, Sandra gazed across the velvety grass of the Domain. She and Nick had sat on this exact same step after they walked through the park that long ago sunny day when Nick had described his secret visit about studying architecture at university, and how he'd paid little attention to the real reason his father sent him. And Sandra had tearfully told Nick of her father's transfer to Randwick.

Ever since that day, she'd promised herself to return to the gallery and find the painting; stand in front of it one more time, re-live the moment when Nick had suddenly said, 'Hold my hand and close your eyes …'

Her sandalled feet made barely a whisper on the parquet floor as she walked quickly through the halls. But not too fast, she

17

decided, as people may be curious – although she badly wanted to run. There was hardly anyone around yet, so she would have the painting all to herself.

With great control, she strolled past the old paintings in their gilded frames, pausing to stand a moment at Gruner's cows in the early morning spring frost. 'Dad's favourite,' Nick had told her. It used to be hers too, but now she had a new favourite … one more room and she would find it …

She imagined Nick taking her hand again, her eyes obediently closed as they walked the few steps to where he'd already glimpsed the picture: seated beside a pool, a young girl threaded red poppies in her long fair hair, daisies in her lap, a golden girdle around her hips. Then he'd said, 'Open your eyes and look at this painting. Who does she remind you of?'

Unable to think of an answer, shaking her head, Sandra stared at the girl who looked so thoughtful, so beautiful, painted so perfectly as if the paint had been licked smooth.

'She reminds me of you,' Nick said. 'Same pretty profile, same hair … and if you wore a long dress like that …' She remembered how she had blushed, brushed off his compliment. It was nothing to do with the sad story of Ophelia, he explained, it was simply how John Waterhouse painted the girl. She could still see the painting clearly in her mind. If she could stand in front of it, feel her hand enclosed in his … this was the room … on the left side, halfway along the wall …

Where the painting had previously hung, there was a picture of a father with a sleeping child. Rapidly she went from room to room, anxious and tearful, but the painting of Ophelia had definitely disappeared. She recalled the little card had said 'on loan from a private collection' – so it must have been returned to hang in the home of its owner – vanished from the gallery.

Outside, Sandra slumped on the steps. It was a stupid idea anyway. Why should the picture have been hanging there, months later? She was a stupid fool to think she could recapture that wonderful day with Nick. Stupid stupid stupid.

It was hard not to cry, and her throat ached with unshed tears. She didn't want to live in the past, as her mother chided her on bleak days when Sandra complained – but the past held her dreams, her memories of all that was lovely. She felt a tear run down her cheek and angrily wiped it away so strangers wouldn't see her distress. Counting one-two-three, she breathed in deeply, tried to calm herself.

More people were arriving at the Gallery, stepping around her where she sat. It must be nearly lunchtime. She stood, dusting the seat of her skirt. Across the road was a kiosk and she bought an icecream in a cone. She would sit there and figure out a melody to play when she got home. It will be a song for Nick, she decided, a song without words in a key full of happiness and hope.

It might begin with morning at Wilga Park, a ripple of notes *andante con brio* like the wind brushing through dry winter grass and paper daisies, and high above, oh, maybe two swallows scooping up pieces of sky. She hummed some experimental notes. Perhaps the key might change ... a discord, a change in beat with the *staccato* stamp of horses' hooves on frosty ground. She smiled to herself ... that might be the easiest part. And finally, a cadence for the peace of evening, the way she remembered shadows lengthening across the fields until daylight faded into darkness.

Forgetting to lick it, her icecream had melted softly into the cone. So easy to say the words, to call her imaginary song *Winter's Day*, but the melody remained elusive, the harmonies would not come.

That night Sandra lay uneasily in her bed, cradling the pillow. So many times she had misted her bedroom mirror with kisses, whispered: I love you Nicholas Morgan. With her eyes closed she could imagine Nick. But it wasn't enough – it was never enough.

Was it wrong to want more of a person, she wondered … when did it become possessive? Ideally we should be like two stars circling about each other, drawn together. A double star? But while Nick stays at Wilga Park he can only be a sun, with me spinning around him, alone on my own orbit.

Five months since she'd watched over him as he lay bruised and sleeping in the hospital. Five months of far-away dreaming on her pillow each night, reliving the touch of his hand on hers at the gallery when she told him her family must leave Curradeen. I will write Nick's song, she promised, and one day soon, I'll take the score out of my handbag and I'll say, 'This is something I wrote especially for you,' and push the pages across the table – yes, we'll be in a café, and instead of picking up the pages immediately, Nick will look at me with so much affection, he'll be so impressed that I wrote a piece for him … he'll finally wake up that I love him, and he'll feel it too, and he'll take my hand and tell me, 'Now I understand, it's been in front of me all the time. I've been in love with you without knowing it, ever since we met that day at the polocrosse.'

The dream was magnificent and Sandra allowed it to flow, Nick close beside her on the pillow, his lips in her hair whispering secrets, loving her, circling like a star, and at last she slept deeply, her arm curled around the pillow.

15 Bentley St., Curradeen.
16 March 1961.

Dear Sandy,

I think you are real brave going to the art gallery by yourself, I would be scared stiff. I suppose you have been to Sydney lots and know where to go. I never went and would get lost on a bus for sure. Did you find your picture, what is it of?

Maybe Mr. L'estrange is Italian like me. If you hear him again on the telephone tell me what he says. Italians say "pronto?" when they answer but I suppose he won't if he dont know whose calling him. He has not got an Italian name but.

I've nearly read all of "The Passage" but Shakespeere is hard and I don't understand any.

Love from Emmy XOX

♩

Seated at the piano at home, Sandra sorted through sheet music to find the Mozart Sonata. At her first lesson Mister L'estrange had announced: 'Nine years old is quite late to begin lessons'. The scalding words still echoed. Music teachers were supposed to be encouraging, so what sort of encouragement was that? 'Hmm, we shall see,' he'd said. Like she was some sort of experiment.

Mozart's dizzying notes flew from her fingers. *Sonata in C Major*, first movement *allegro*, try to keep every note pure, bright... a blur of semi-quavers, this bar *fortissimo* – all these darned grace notes diddle-diddle-diddle. Principal Theme *andante*... Oops. Why did she have to learn this stupid piece, impossible to put her heart into it.

She'd rather practise her own songs, threading them among the set study pieces, surprised that her mother never seemed to notice. Prue sometimes teased, mimicking her songs until Sandra drowned her voice with a loud set of scales or crashing bass chords. And in her dreams, Nick stood close beside her at the keyboard, turning the pages as she played.

Nick Nick Nicholas Nick … she hadn't hummed his name like that since they moved to Sydney. It had disappeared on the endless seven hour train journey, changed by the rhythm of the wheels to a click click clickety click. Nick was at home at Wilga Park. Perhaps as he got used to a wheelchair and regained his strength, he would forget her … but that was too too sad to think about.

Concentrate on Mozart: Secondary Theme … *pianissimo* … those trills were not crisp enough. Would he recall that she'd visited him in hospital? In the midnight dimness of the ward, she had leaned over his bed, pressed her lips to Nick's forehead in the precise spot where his own lips had kissed her. His eyelids had opened briefly, closed again. Did he recognize her?

Only the nurse knew she was there – the nurse who'd found her searching for him on the third night, and told her Nick had been sent to Sydney for surgery. She hadn't seen him again.

She heaved a deep breath. Last page … together she and Nick were riding their horses, the wind tossing manes and tails, Nick smiling beside her, cheeks flushed, brown hair blown back from his face as he leaned forward into a gallop. When they came to the steepest drops, the other riders fell back, leaving Nick the only one, the bravest one, shirt flapping as he disappeared into the distance with the final fortissimo chords.

Angela came to the door, wiping her hands on an apron. 'That sounded very nice from the kitchen,' she said. 'Finish up now, dinner's on the table.'

Her father and Prue were already seated. Angela continued, 'Tomorrow you'll have to start your practice earlier so you don't run into meal time.'

Don smiled a hello as he sliced his pork chop. 'Pass the apple sauce, please,' was all he said.

Sandra wondered why her father was so quiet lately. He used to talk to them about his day in the office, stories about some of the customers, the odd reasons some people gave for wanting a loan – not that he ever told any names. One man even wanted to start a fish farm! When she asked her mother, Angela said he was weary from his new job and Sandra thought it was probably true. But an earlier companionship between them all was missing.

Last winter, bundled into the car to travel the fifteen miles to Denalbo polocrosse field had been very special – even mugs of tea on the sidelines were joyous, cheering the game and talking to whoever was there. Especially Nick and the Morgans. And Lofty, whose family owned the farm next door, who'd been such a pest at school. Was it possible she missed Lofty, too?

Now that they lived in Randwick, the household seemed to have become quieter. They still watched television together after dinner, seated on the brand new lounge suite, Ginger curled on Don's lap. *Rawhide* remained a favourite and Don whistled through his teeth as usual until Angela said, 'Shush.'

The pile of magazines and books in the newspaper rack beside Angela's chair grew and grew. She wanted a job in a florist shop to help her decide about a business of her own, and every night a book lay open on her lap, or the classified pages from the *Herald*, with circles drawn around relevant advertisements.

Prue had abandoned learning to knit. It was too hot and sticky, she complained. Happy at school, some weekends she stayed overnight at a girl friend's house. 'We have midnight feasts,' she skited to Sandra. 'My friends have got hundreds of records.'

'They have not,' Sandra said sourly, but envious of the possibility.

Prue ignored the rebuke. 'My favourite's *Boom Boom Baby*. Crash Craddock's sooo good looking.'

'I don't care.'

'He sings that his baby did the chicken in the middle of the room. What's the chicken?'

Sandra knew her companionship with Prue was slipping away. There were times when she missed how they used to ride their bikes to the creek, or drew pictures together, making up stories. But most of all she missed Emilia, missed all those afternoons after school, sitting on Emilia's bed talking about everything and nothing, and at the weekends whizzing around the roller-skating rink or lazing in the warm grass at the old cemetery.

At her new school, next to the confident city girls, she felt like a country bumpkin who would never fit in, with nothing to say of any interest to anyone. No matter how she dressed or how she did her hair, it never looked right. Maybe she should get a perm like some of the girls in her class? She tried to picture what she might look like with really curly hair, but when she brushed it thoroughly and wound it in a plait, she was glad for the thick weight of it. Nick had called her 'my pretty piano player', so why change what he liked?

Meredith developed a suspicion that all was not as well as it should be, and often suggested that on Saturday mornings she and Sandra make an excursion into the city shops, or to Rowe Street to discover what was new in the art studios and decorators' windows.

On these days, thanks to auntie, Sandra returned home feeling better.

23 Tyrell St., Randwick, N.S.W.,
19th March, 1961.

Dear Emmy,

I said I'd write with more news and here it is! No, I didn't find the painting and I searched in all the rooms. It was loaned to the gallery so it must've been given back. I saw it with Nick, and he said I looked like the girl in the picture. I was sad not to see it again but I'm all right now.

I had a lovely time with Aunt Meredith yesterday, we went to the tea room where I went with Nick, then we went to David Jones and pretended to buy hats. Auntie took all the pins out of her French roll so she could try one with net that came down over her eyes and looked so beautiful. She has red hair, I think maybe she dyes it.

Auntie is really glamorous and not at all like Dad. She told me she used to dance the tango at the Trocadero which is a dance hall in the middle of Sydney. Her boyfriend was in the army! I worked out she's 32, I wonder why she never got married. Sometimes I think it'd be good to be like her when I grow up. All I would do is study piano and play in concerts and travel the world. Mum says I'm selfish when I tell her that.

It's Easter next week, hooray! We're having an Easter egg hunt in our garden. On Sunday we're going to the Royal Easter Show and I wish you could come too.

Do you think your parents would let me stay with you in the May holidays? I would come on the train.

Love from Sandra xxxxx

15 Bentley St., Curradeen.
Saturday, 25th March, 1961.

Dear Sandy,

You can come and stay, thats real good and Pa can't ask me to work in the shop if your here.

Guess what, Nick came in the shop today with Mrs Morgan and I got to serve them. She bought Easter eggs. He is a bit bent and has two walking sticks. I thought you would like to know. We go to Mass lots over Easter. The best bit is Nonna makes special bocconotti bikkies, made of pastry filled with armands and cherry jam and with icing on.

I wish I had an auntie like yours. When my relatives visit us they all talk so fast and shout at me Emeeeeelia! Ora parla italiano! I think my auntie and uncle dont like me because I don't understand them. I was born in Australia and at home I talk how my family talks.

Nonna knits all day with a black scarf on her head and a skirt down to her ankles. She doesn't know English but it doesn't matter. I like it when she sits in the shop with me. This week my brothers, Nonna and me helped Mamma make tomato sauce with hundreds of real ripe tomatoes, we take the skins off with hot water and after its all boiled up with Pa's onions and garlic and herbs we squash it into jars. I like that part best. Mamma is going to put some in the shop to sell.

I'm so excited your coming to visit, we all miss you, Mamma, Pa, and my 2 silly brothers.

Love from Emmy xxx

23 Tyrell St., Randwick.
3rd. April, 1961.

Dear Emmy,

I booked my train ticket and I'm counting down till I leave. We'll have 5 whole days to do what we like. Can we borrow another bike and ride to the cemetery like we used to and I can visit Miss Brooks too? I'm glad I won't be here because the kitchen is going to be painted and Mum has to put everything away. Prue wants to help, she's such a goody-goody when she wants to be.

I am so happy that you saw Nick. I want to know more. What does he really look like, you said he needs sticks to walk.

Did he say anything? What did Mrs Morgan say or did she just buy Easter eggs? Tell me everything, pleeeeeeeeeeeeease.

The Show was good fun and we got some sample bags. I got very sun burnt and we sucked lots of ice blocks to keep cool. The grand parade was enormous, I liked the horses best. In the cat pavillion some of the cats are so beautiful it's lucky Ginger doesn't know he's only a plain "domestic short-haired tabby." Prue spent all her pocket money on rides and she ate so much fairy floss she vomited last night.

Only one month to go!

Lots of Love from Sandra xxxxxxO

15 Bentley St., Curradeen.
15th April, 61.

Dear Sandy,

I posted your birthday present this week plus Nonna knitted you a surprise!

My grandpa died on Wednesday. We are all very sad. I went to school but Pa came to get me. The funeral was yesterday and we put roses and white lilies on his grave.

We will be at the station to meet your train. Nonna said you will help us to smile again. I will write more next time.

Love from Emmy xxx

23 Tyrell St, Randwick.
20th April, 61.

Dearest Emmy,

I know you must be very sad your grandpa died. I hope you liked the card Mum sent. I wanted to write my own letter and tell you that I think of you every day, and wish I still lived at Curradeen but I'll soon be there.

Thank you for the box of lace hankies with your pretty card. I got it today on my birthday! Please tell your Nonna thank you for the scarf, it's so long it must have taken ages to knit. We ate some of your biscotti last night and I cried in bed again. Carol is O.K. I suppose, she still sits with me but I don't know if it's because she likes me or because she was told to.

Big disaster! Mum saw Mr. L'estrange in the butcher shop yesterday and saw his earring and she says it's wrong for a man to wear earrings and she wants me to change to another tutor. She can't do that when I am starting to do well and I even play Mozart better. I really want him to be my teacher now.

Aunt Meredith has invited us for dinner again so I better get ready. Try not to be too sad.

> *Love and kisses from your friend*
> *Sandra XXXX*

With Sympathy

Dear Mrs. Ferrari,

We are very sorry to hear about the loss of your father. Our thoughts are with you and your family and we extend our deepest sympathy to you all.

> *Yours sincerely,*
> *Angela Abbott and family.*

23 Tyrell St.,
Randwick, N.S.W.
20th April, 1961.

Dear Miss Brooks,

*I'm writing to let you know that I will be staying with
my friend Emilia Ferrari in the May holidays and I would
like to come and visit you.*

*You will be pleased to know that I am studying Handel
Suite No.14 in G, and Nocturne in B flat by John Field for
the exam. I also have to learn Mozart Sonata in C major
K279 for the exam later this year.*

*I wish you were still my teacher, my new tutor is a man
but I liked you much better. I hope I can see you when I visit
Curradeen.*

Yours sincerely,
Sandra Abbott.

15 Bentley St.,
Curradeen, N.S.W.
28th April, 1961.

Dear Sandy,

Your mum's card is very nice. Its sad my grandpa isn't
around any more. Nonna teached me to knit and I am making
a scarf. It's a bit crooked but I like that I made it. It's better than
reading comics.

Pa has dug the hugest vegetable garden and drives the
truck around to houses where people can't go out to shop,
mostly old people. He made a sign for our front fence "Ferrari's
Farm". I know its not a proper big farm but the sign is nice.

Lofty says he wants to be called by his real name. His real
name is "Warwick". He is taller than me now so he's not "lofty"
anymore. Its hard to change as everyone called him Lofty,
teachers too.

There is a new boy called Roger, he's nice. Third Year is
better than Second maybe because some kids want to leave

after the Intermediate to get a job (like Tony) and they are feeling grown up. Pa wants me to leave at the end of the year and help him in the shop but Mamma and Nonna say no.

We had our social this week and I can dance the Pride of Erin proper now. I asked Lofty for lady's choice. I'm not going with Lofty but I like him because he's fun and he doesn't call me fat dago like some of the kids.

You will be here next week and we will have a real good time.

Love from Emmy XXX

three.

As they drove past the Town Hall on the way from the Curradeen railway station, Sandra recalled the dizzy excitement of that wonderful winter night at the concert. The cheers after her performance, the audience shouting *Bravo!* Later, she had stood with her bouquet of flowers, and Mrs Morgan had kissed her and Nick held her hand for a moment, then at his mother's suggestion he'd kissed her cheek. And now, here she was, back again for a few precious days.

Enveloped in hugs and kisses, Sandra was given the warmest, loveliest hug from Emilia and big smacking kisses on both cheeks from Mr and Mrs Ferrari and Emilia's tiny grandmother, *la signora* Puglisi, who flapped her hands excitedly, insisting that Sandra please call her nonna, *per favore*. Mrs Ferrari looked her up and down, and with enthusiasm announced: 'Ooh, you growing up so pretty!' The two little brothers hung back, but were no longer so little.

Emilia also had changed in six months: still plump but grown taller, somehow smoothing out the puppy fat of childhood, giving her an unexpected gloss – no more the shy girl from Second Year. Emilia looked beautiful to Sandra, who decided that her own mirror at home told lies, regardless of what her mother said about growing up.

For dinner that evening, Nonna cooked an enormous meat pie, with homemade tomato sauce and vegetables from the garden. Mr Ferrari spoke less English than Emilia's mother, and he and his mother-in-law chatted above everyone else, Nonna's voice so high and cracked, making Sandra giggle with Emilia, because they had no idea what Nonna was saying amidst the usual noise of everyone talking at once.

Mrs Ferrari laughed too. 'When he talks to his vegetables, he don't speak English – they all speak Italian, *tutti parlano italiano!* And she laughed loudly so that talk erupted again at the Italian end of the table and Sandra could only smile and eat her pie.

For a while Sandra and Emilia whispered in bed together, then Sandra sensed that Emilia was asleep, breathing gently beside her on the pillows. One day soon they were going to ride their bikes to Wilga Park for a surprise visit, and surely Nick would guess how she felt about him.

Emilia borrowed an extra bicycle and early next morning they rode along River Street in the direction of the old cemetery. There they wandered among the many graves of pioneers of the district; inscriptions carved on headstones told stories of deaths following old age or disease, the influenza epidemic taking babies and elderly people at random.

Sandra stopped at a headstone marked *Emma Louisa Smith 1917 – 1919*. 'Emmy Lou died of the flu,' she sang. 'Remember?'

Emilia turned away from the baby's grave. 'I like the one better that says "He was a kind man and not forgotten,"' she said. 'Do you want to see Angus's grave?'

They trod the grassy pathways among unnamed mounds, broken crosses, rusted iron railings and elaborate memorials, until they came to the new, well-mown section, the plain granite headstone: *Angus Burns – Abide with me – 1941 – 1960*.

'His grave always has a posy on it,' Emilia said. 'I guess it's from his mother.'

Sandra traced a finger along the letters. Once upon a time, she'd hated him: for his blunt manner, the rough way he'd tried to kiss her at the Morgans' party. But ultimately she had recognized the deep loss his death caused the family, to Nick; the huge vacancy in their lives. In her heart, she knew forgiveness was far better than hate. The last time she went to see his grave, Emilia had followed her, and they'd sat shoulder to shoulder, leaning against the stone, with nothing to say anymore that had not already been said.

'Every Sunday Mamma and Nonna come to visit Nonno's grave. Sometimes I come too.' Emilia led Sandra unerringly along the paths until they came to the grave of her grandfather.

A marble slab covered where he lay. An elaborate, carved headstone embedded with a picture frame held the old man's photograph: Franco Puglisi. Imitation white roses bunched in a vase decorated the tomb.

Emilia sat on the slab, stroked the photograph. 'I hate that he's down there underground, but he's in heaven now with the angels, and we should be happy he's at peace. It was sad when he didn't know who he was any more.' She read aloud the inscription, rolling the Italian words as if her tongue held a jelly baby, '*Vivrai per sempre nei nostri cuori*. It means you will always live in our hearts.'

Sandra gazed at the unexpected novelty of the dead man's picture, aged years younger. Although once she might have argued: I don't believe in angels, or heaven and hell – today she knew it was better, kinder, to be quiet, and leave Emmy and her nonno undisturbed. 'That's lovely,' she murmured.

The cemetery was deserted: a sunny morning, occasional birds winging through trees and sky, insects chirring invisibly in the grass. Emilia jiggled the roses into position, fixing the vase so it wouldn't tip over, as Sandra plucked stalks of encroaching grass away from the marble. Every hour that passed was bringing her closer to Nick, and soon she became restless, wanting to leave. She waited until Emilia looked satisfied with her flower arrangement, then said, 'Will we go past Miss Brooks' house and maybe knock on her door to see if she's home?'

They cycled along the narrow back roads to where Miss Brooks' cottage and all the other identical weatherboard cottages perched on a small rise, safe from floodwaters from the distant river. The lawn needed mowing and rampant yellow dandelions grew along the brick path to the front door. Silence blanketed the little house.

A hollowness swept Sandra's heart as she knocked on the door. Surely Miss Brooks would be at home today. She knocked again. No answering footsteps. Miss Brooks' cottage was firmly locked.

At the front gate, Sandra peeked in the letterbox. Her letter from two weeks ago was still there. She took it, turned it over. Snails had eaten most of the envelope, rendering it into paper lace like a doily in a cake shop. It was unbearably sad. Folding the remains of her letter, she pushed it deep into her pocket.

After breakfast the following day, sitting side by side on Emilia's bed, Sandra broached the topic she was so keen to talk about. 'Now we've got our bicycles, can we ride out to Wilga Park this morning?'

Emilia frowned. 'It's miles from here and then we've got to ride all the way back again.'

'But Nick can drive us home,' Sandra pleaded. How could Emilia go back on the plan – she'd written it in her letter, hadn't she? And Emmy hadn't said No.

'No,' Emilia said flatly. 'I don't want to. It's too far and it'll take all day.'

'But I thought you'd like to.'

'*You'd* like to. You only told me you wanted to visit Miss Brooks.'

'Don't be such a meanie … you know how I feel about Nick.'

'I'm not a meanie,' Emilia protested, bouncing on the bed. 'You came to visit me, didn't you, not Nick?'

'But I've come all this way … I sat for hours and hours in the train—'

'So? There's lots we can do without going to Wilga Park. Nick may not even be there. We can go skating and to the pictures, we can say hello if we see Lofty—'

Sandra's voice rose an octave, '*Lofty!* My only chance to see Nick and you don't want to!' For a moment she simmered, then jumped to her feet, fingers opening and closing with despair and sudden fury. 'Oooh, I never knew you could be so unkind and *selfish*. You never used to be like this, we used to do everything together …' Searching for more hurtful words, she glared at Emilia. 'You've got so selfish, one day your heart will just shrivel up and it'll serve you right! No wonder Tony never liked you, he never even noticed you because you were fat and ugly. And *mean*!'

Emilia gave a screech, clapping her hands over her mouth.

From the kitchen, Mrs Ferrari heard the squabble. She appeared at the bedroom door, wagged a warning finger. 'This is very bad, friends fighting,' she told them. 'Sandy, I hear the very terrible thing you say about Emilia's heart. You say sorry, *per favore!*'

Stunned at her own outburst, Sandra cried through sudden tears, 'I'm sorry, I'm sorry, I don't know why I said that. I'm sorry, Emmy.'

Mrs Ferrari remained in the doorway, dark eyebrows drawn together. '*Ti metti prima*, always you put yourself first … is no good.'

Sandra had never seen her angry before, not even cross, and she was dismayed.

'No ride to see Nick,' Mrs Ferrari scolded. 'You come to see Emilia. *Solo* Emilia.' With the last stern remark and another wag of her finger, she left them alone.

'I didn't mean it, or what I said about Tony,' Sandra tried.

'Yes, you did. I can't believe you said those nasty things.'

Sandra bit her tongue on more bitter words. She rattled her brain to think… Emilia had always brushed aside the rude things that kids said, so she'd soon forget the argument. But what could she say now to make it better?

'Will we go down the street? We can get a milkshake or an icecream. I'll buy you any flavour you like. We can walk up and down like we used to, and look at the shops. Maybe we'll see Lofty?'

Without looking at Sandra, Emilia tidied her bed. She smoothed her skirt, put on her flatties. Her voice trembled, 'All right then, before I change my mind.'

Curradeen's main street looked exactly the same. Sandra stood outside the newsagency, staring across the road to the impersonal bank building and her old bedroom window where she had secretly watched for Nick Morgan to arrive in town. All those Saturday mornings that she'd galloped down the stairs, feigning calm as she sauntered into the newsagent. Each time she promised herself that today she would smile… and always she'd frozen.

So many memories. Now she wouldn't see Nick at all, and soon she would be going home.

As they walked to the café, she searched despondently for familiar faces. After the gloss of the city department stores and boutiques, the main street looked dull, even a little shabby, the window displays old-fashioned.

Suddenly Emilia gave her a sharp nudge with her elbow… and Sandra was amazed to see Nick and his mother strolling towards them, already smiling. Mrs Morgan in a lightweight suit, carried a large, boxy handbag; Nick in tweedy sports coat, felt hat tipped to one side, held a long walking stick in each hand for support. Emilia's description was right, Nick was bent.

But unbelievably, it was Nick! Heart thumping, she bit her lip as they approached.

'My dear Sandra,' Beth Morgan said. 'Goodness me, what a surprise. Is your family here too?'

Sandra ached to look first at Nick, but with a great effort, kept her eyes politely on Mrs Morgan. 'Only me. I came on the train,' she explained. 'I'm staying with Emilia till the day after tomorrow.'

'Hello girls,' Nick said. 'How are you, Sandra? Enjoying a visit to our illustrious town?'

'Now, now Nick, we have a very nice town. Don't embarrass the girls.'

Sandra faced him: tall and lean, grey-green eyes, soft brown hair beneath his hat, but instead of his usual riding boots, he wore stout lace-ups. She carefully avoided focussing on his two metal props and the heavy shoes but Nick saw her gaze sweep across him, no matter how hard she tried to hide it.

'I'm still a bit of a mess,' he grimaced. 'I need good foot support while I'm swinging around on these sticks.'

'You've made great progress,' his mother chimed in. She regarded Sandra kindly. 'He was six months in a wheelchair and now look at him. In no time at all he'll be able to throw those crutches away.'

'That's good,' Sandra managed. 'That's really good. How's Toffee?'

'It's all good news for Toffee,' Nick laughed. 'She found herself a big, solid stallion called *Spirit*, our neighbour's horse. I don't know how they did it; I thought she was just getting fat and lazy the last couple of matches. She's got a week old filly that looks just like her.'

'Oh, gosh, that's lovely. What's her name?'

'I haven't come up with a name yet. Maybe you can think of one?'

Mrs Morgan touched Nick's arm to interrupt, looked apologetically at Sandra and Emilia. 'I'm sorry, we have to rush. We're getting the plane to Melbourne.'

'I have regular physiotherapy,' Nick said. 'We stay with Mum's folks a few days, then fly home again.'

'We must go, dear. Harry's waiting in the car. Give my love to your mother and tell her it was lovely to hear from her, I'm sorry I haven't replied.'

Her mother wrote to Mrs Morgan and never said a word? How could she do that without telling her? Her brain was whirring. Names, names, names for the foal!

Suddenly Mrs Morgan was planting a kiss on Sandra's cheek, and for one magical, beautiful, perfect moment, Nick leaned towards her and kissed her forehead, right where he'd kissed her when they said goodbye in Sydney last year. She lifted her face to him, kissed his cheek, felt his shaven skin beneath her lips, wanted his arms to be around her, holding her close.

The name burst out unbidden, miraculously: '*Honey!*' Sandra cried. 'You could call the foal Honey. '

Nick gave a thumbs up. 'You beauty! That's perfect for a sweet little foal with a mother called Toffee. And she is a honey too.'

Then they were gone, headed towards a car parked across the road. Harry Morgan waved a greeting out the window. Sandra felt a secret satisfaction that Nick hadn't kissed Emilia too.

'See,' Emilia said. 'They wouldn't have been at home if we'd gone there on our bikes.'

Sandra looked sideways at Emilia but the smile returned to her was weak and watery. She knew she'd badly hurt her friend and that the hurt lingered.

For Sandra, their argument had quickly faded, cancelled by the joy of seeing Nick. It didn't matter that it was only for a few minutes. If they hadn't seen him right then, by marvellous coincidence, she would have left town with no knowledge of where or how he was. And she'd named Nick's foal, a little chestnut filly just like Toffee.

7

> 23 Tyrell St., Randwick, N.S.W.
> 13th May, '61.

Dear Mrs. Ferrari,

Thank you very much for having me to stay. It was lovely to be back and I had such a nice time. I miss Emilia and all your family and it was very nice of you to let me stay. I even liked weeding and digging Mr. Ferrari's garden. Please thank him for the long bean seeds which I gave to my mother.

> *With love from Sandra.*

> 23 Tyrell St., Randwick.
> 13th May, 61.

Dearest Emmy,

I feel so far away now, when all the things I really like are miles away. You are my best and dearest and only real friend, and I'm sorry I said awful things and called you names.

Your family is lovely and your mother was very kind to me when I cried that night. That was two sad things, and finding out Miss Brooks had gone and she never got my letter.

I wanted to see Nick so badly and I'm sorry I got cross because you wouldn't ride our bikes out to Morgan's place. I know Nick would've driven us home in his ute. It was very lucky we saw them in town.

Please give your Nonna a hug too, because even though we couldn't chat, tell her I practise the words she told me every day! Bon Gorrrno. Bonner Notta! Arriva derrrchy! I know I can't spell it.

A big hug and love from
Sandra, your friend forever oxoxoxo

"Ferrari's Farm,"
20th May, 61.

Dear Sandra,

I was very sad when you visited because I thought you wanted to see me, and all the time you only wanted to see Nick. You never wrote you wanted to ride our bikes to the farm. I was glad he went to Melbourne and we had a nicer time when you found that out.

I thought I was your best friend but really you like Nick better. I know you were being unkind because of all that. I will give Nonna your hug.

From Emilia.

26th May, 61.

Dear Emilia,

Our pact for best friends forever was excluding boys. I said I was sorry.

From Sandra.

23 Tyrell St, Randwick..
12th June, 61.

Dearest Emmy,

I miss getting your letters. We've been best friends since 4th class and I still want to be your friend. I've been unhappy most of this year and I can't help it when sometimes I'm rude. I know what I said to you was really bad. You're not fat and ugly, you look beautiful now and I'm sorry sorry sorry.

I'm writing this on the Queen's Birthday holiday Monday. There's a polocrosse carnival this weekend and I'm so sad that we can't go. There is nothing for me to do here. I play piano lots but that's different. Thank goodness for Auntie.

Please write and tell me we can be friends again.
Love from your lonely friend,
Sandra xxx

"Ferrari's Farm,"
15 Bentley St., Curradeen.
20th June, 61.

Dear Sandy,

I want to be best friends again. It was a horrid feeling when I thought we would never ever see each other again. I talked to my mother and she said wait about two weeks and you would write to me again and she was right.

Nonna gave me your letter when I got home from school and she was very happy too. I love my Nonna living with us. I finished my scarf, I have got real fast knitting now. It's school colours so I can wear it to school when its really cold, like now.

Pa gave Roger a job to dig our garden bigger because he takes vegies to lots more people now. On cracker night he helped Pa build a bonfire and they lit sky rockets, the best was roman candles and catherine wheels. My brothers threw jumping jacks at me till Roger chased them. He is very nice for a boy but I like Warwick better.

41

Mr. Wilkins went to another school, I bet because he didn't teach very good. We have a new lady teacher.

Love from Emmy XOX

23 Tyrell St., Randwick,
28 / 6 / 61.

Dear Emmy,

I'm very happy you still want to be my friend. I hope your birthday present arrives before the 8th, I hope it fits and you like the colour. Will you have a party? I wish I could be there again. Your cracker night sounds fun, we watched fireworks in our street and there were loud bangs all around.

Our winter uniform is a navy tunic and blazer with tights, which is better than stockings, and I like my navy hat. We have to wear an ugly blue and yellow striped tie and we're supposed to wear gloves but most girls don't. Nobody talks to me much and I eat my sandwiches on a seat by myself. If I complain Mum says I have to make more effort to be friendly and smile when people look at me. I would look like an idiot.

Carol invited me to her birthday party last Sunday, I gave her pearl pink nail varnish. I didn't tell anyone I had my birthday already but they asked. When I told them they laughed like mad and said that's Hitler's birthday too. I wish I could take back my present.

I sit my music exam this Saturday. I hope I do all right, the result gets sent to Mr. L'estrange.

Love from Sandra

xxxxxxxxxxxxxxxxxxxxx

P.S. I like "Ferrari's Farm" for your vegetable garden.

four.

Sandra spread her Geography homework on the dining table: black Indian ink, mapping pen and coloured pencils. How ridiculous and irrelevant to be asked to draw a map of Africa's mineral deposits. She could hear the rapid d-d-d-d-d of her mother's sewing machine in the next room. That would be the flannelette pyjamas for her and her sister. Hopefully hers wouldn't be yellow with stupid mice like last winter.

She looked at Prue, curled in an armchair with a *Three Musketeers* comic.

'Does Mum know you went to the Stadium last Saturday afternoon?' She had wanted to ask since she'd spied Prue with a group of girls last weekend on the footpath outside the Sydney Stadium, but she wanted her parents to be out of hearing.

Prue looked startled. 'How did you know?'

'I saw you when Auntie and I drove past.'

'Please don't tell Mum," Prue pleaded. 'It's fun, and I'm with other girls.'

'How can you like going there with a crowd of rough people?'

'They're not. And how would you know, you've never been.'

'And I don't want to.'

'Will you tell?'

'No. You'd get into too much trouble, and you'll spoil it for me going out with Aunt Meredith. Mum already doesn't like it, I don't know why.'

She finished colouring the diamond and gold deposits in two different shades of blue, with an orange patch for bauxite.

Prue peered over Sandra's shoulder at the map. 'You should've done yellow for the gold.'

'Go away. I don't need your help.'

The sewing machine fell silent. 'What are you two whispering about?' Angela came in, pyjamas draped over one arm. 'I'll need you both to try these on, for the length.' She inspected the map of Africa. 'Why didn't you use more colours, make it pretty? Better finish up now, Sandy, it's time for practice.'

'I'm nearly finished,' Sandra said to her mother's retreating back. 'Two more minutes.' Irritated, she grumbled to herself: why does she have to remind me – I've never forgotten, even once. But she's got to announce it every day like a wind-up toy: time to get up, time to practise, time for dinner, time for bed, blah-blah blah-de-blah-blah.

Flipping her comic, Prue lingered by the table. Face inscrutable, she said, 'Come with me this Saturday arvo?' When Sandra didn't answer she added, 'it costs six shilling and we sit in the bleachers up the back, and the stage goes round in a circle—'

'I said I don't want to,' Sandra placed her pencils one by one in their box. 'Why would I want to go to that old tin shed, and you say everyone screams so loudly you can't hear a thing, so what for?' Truthfully, she wondered what it might be like. She knew that boys roamed around at interval, looking at girls, and once Prue had dropped her purse down below the seats and had to get a guard help her retrieve it.

Practice finished, her fingers found new notes to experimentally trickle onto the keyboard, a melodic progression of tones, intervals and chords with a pleasing harmony. But what if she didn't want harmony, but wanted something to reflect her life right now: the upheaval, the lurch her heart gave at seeing Nick, the heartbreak of farewell and emptiness. She tried again, debating the key – G major or C minor? Oh, it was impossible.

She shut the piano lid rather more heavily than she meant to, annoyed that her new song wasn't working. Taking blank paper and pencil, she went into her bedroom, with the hope that the elusive song would come to her, oblivious to her mother's voice calling her to dinner.

On Saturday mornings, Angela liked to investigate her list of florist shops, and Prue either went with her, or to a friend's house. Don never got home from the bank until after it closed at midday. Always a perfect opportunity, Sandra thought, to go out with Aunt Meredith.

Sometimes they drove to Leichhardt's 'Little Italy', as Meredith called it, where they sat at a café with coffee and a crispy sweet ricotta-filled cannoli or a gelato each, experimenting with new and delicious flavours while surrounded by a hubbub of voices. Sandra was surprised at the easy way her aunt flirted with the waiters, who flirted back with genuine smiles. 'Part of their profession,' Meredith explained to Sandra with a wink.

Or they might drive to Double Bay and amid the bustle of the harbour-side village, they would trawl the boutiques where small women with intricate lacquered hairstyles did their best to persuade Meredith that she was absolutely divine, and that Sandra would appear perfectly gorgeous in this or that dress, none of which they ever bought.

On such days, whizzing about in Meredith's old car, she could almost feel at home in the city. But really, she suspected it was simply being with Meredith.

One Saturday, while brushing her hair at the dressing table mirror in Meredith's bedroom, Sandra noticed a new picture among the family photographs.

She peered closely at it, picked it up, fingered the scalloped frame. In a black and white print, the steady gaze of a man stared back at her: good looking, a strong symmetrical face with a cheerful smile. He stood beside a car, his hand resting on the door as if he was about to leave. Aunt Meredith's car! She turned over the frame, read the inscription: *Austinmer, 1950*. Who was he, and where had his photo been for years?

So... I'm not the only one with secrets. Sandra replaced the picture at the exact angle in which it had stood. Auntie has another secret.

When she came out of the bedroom, Meredith glanced at her with a knowing smile. 'You saw the photograph, of course?'

Although a rush of questions had gathered while Sandra looked at the picture, she repeated, 'Of course.' Auntie would tell her, if only she could be patient.

Angela didn't often go into Meredith's bedroom, but how long before she spotted a new photograph among the family faces on the dressing table, and full of curiosity, present her own set of questions to her sister-in-law?

The following weekend Sandra had her chance.

'Auntie—' she began.

But Meredith interrupted her. 'I know, you're going to ask me about the photo,' she said, setting out place mats for their lunch. 'If you wait quietly, I'll tell you. It's taken me six years to put that photograph on my dressing table, so it might take me a while to tell you the story. All right?'

Sandra nodded, silently and obediently carrying spoons and plates to the dining room.

'Sit yourself down, Sandra, and I'll be with you in a minute.'

She heard Meredith fossicking among the records and presently the crisp notes of a piano drifted through the house.

'Bach's *Sarabande*...' Meredith set bowls of pea soup on the table, shook open her serviette. 'Bread?' She passed the basket of rolls to Sandra. 'I believe Glenn Gould *hums* while he plays and studios have great trouble recording his music without any odd noises.'

Sandra listened to the precise, pure notes. It was obviously going to take a long while to hear even the *beginning* of Meredith's story. At this rate, they'd be sitting at the table till dark.

Finally, Meredith gathered up the empty bowls and plates. 'I think we'll go down to the seaside for a walk—'

'But we've—'

'Hush. I'll tell you the story with my toes in the sand and the wind in my hair,' Meredith said emphatically. 'Otherwise, I'll find it difficult. But you're old enough to hear, and who knows, you may even have some understanding.'

This surprised Sandra. Understanding Aunt Meredith? Long ago, she'd heard her mother trying to prise answers out of her father, but he'd closed up like a trap. Perhaps her auntie's secret was too terrible to speak about. So they would go down to the beach at Bronte, and she would listen quietly. This, she promised herself, because Aunt Meredith had said that maybe she would understand.

Meredith pulled a beret over her hair. 'Bring your jacket,' she said. 'It'll be chilly.'

Below the ocean pool, the sea frothed and swirled. A lazy swell on a low tide kept the waves from breaking over the concrete wall, and they leaned their elbows on the iron railing. Meredith hadn't spoken much, except to say that she liked the beach in winter. Sandra leaned beside her, watching the waves wash in and out: now splashing high over the rocks, now drawing back to reveal clinging winkles and limpets. Any remaining oysters had long ago been picked clean by intrepid foragers. She heard the claw-click of a hidden crab, and peering down into the gloom, pondered what else might be nudging around the bottom of the sea, close by, in sunken weeds. Wobbegongs and slimy octopus! Deeply dark, unfathomable, on this winter day the ocean contained all melancholy, stretching to infinity.

And still, Meredith didn't speak.

They left the ocean pool and wandered to the firm sand above the tide line. Lumps of seaweed had been torn from the sea and washed ashore by a recent storm, and the smell was strong and salty. An occasional seagull poked among the debris. Sandra wished her aunt would get to the story.

As if she was a mind-reader, Meredith gave a half smile. 'His name was William. Sometimes we'd sit here on the beach long after the sun went down, until the sand got too cold.

'Your story about Nick reminded me of when I met Will. You were fourteen, I was fifteen. Perhaps that's why I sensed how you felt when you came to Sydney and met Nick for that one perfect day in the city. Am I right?'

Sandra nodded. 'Yes, perhaps.'

'It's when you feel that you love someone very much and yet circumstances prevent anything more happening. Your family moved to Sydney, and my William joined the army.'

'But Nick was so badly injured—'

'I know that, but the immediate result is the same: you said goodbye and so did I. But for me, the end result was quite different.

'I met William at the pictures one day when he was on leave – he was with a girl I knew and I was with a friend. We liked each other immediately. Will was eighteen when he enlisted in the army – late in 1944 – just in time for the end of the war as it turned out. He'd wanted to fight in the jungle division. I didn't want him going to any jungle to fight the Japanese, so I was thrilled when I heard people saying the war might soon be over.

'William was from a very wealthy family. Industrialists. About a year after the war ended, his parents and his sister died in an accident—'

Sandra drew in a breath. 'An accident! What sort of accident?'

'A light plane. His father was the pilot. 'Eventually . . . ' she paused as if remembering that sad day. 'William inherited everything.'

By now they'd reached the end of the small beach and turned to walk into the park. 'Let's sit out of the wind for a while,' Meredith said. 'It's blowing off the south pole.'

Sandra squeezed onto the wooden bench beside Meredith. 'What about my father? I know he didn't go to war.'

'No, the bank wouldn't release him. I think secretly he was relieved. Donald was several years older than me and engaged to your mother.'

'Did they ever meet William?'

'Donald did, when our parents were trying to get me to stop seeing him. We'd plan to go to the cinema separately, because they didn't approve of me meeting a boy after dark. So I'd go with my conniving girlfriend and we'd meet our boyfriends in the foyer. It was great fun. After the pictures sometimes we'd sit in the park and watch the searchlights sweeping across the sky.'

'You were sneaky,' Sandra laughed. 'Like me, when I met Nick in Sydney without anyone finding out.

'Similar … but the roof fell in when William quit the army, and I turned seventeen and left home to live with him.'

Golly Gosh! Sandra had never heard of anyone running away from home to live with a man.

'My father wouldn't give permission for me to marry,' Meredith continued. 'He called Will a wastrel, a layabout, and worse things, so I packed my suitcase and left. We spent a year in Brisbane, far away from my worrisome parents.'

'So, where did you go after that?'

'William sold the big family home and bought us a lovely place, which finally he gave to me – where I live now.'

Sandra was incredulous. She wanted to ask, how could William just give away a house? Meredith's home … no wonder her parents didn't talk about Meredith's past – maybe they didn't know the secret. She opened her mouth to ask a question, but Meredith shook her head.

'Ah, maybe that's enough for today. Anyway, it's getting late and it really is very cold. Your mother will be wondering where we've got to.' Her eyes showed dark circles beneath. 'I'll get into trouble,' she laughed, without humour. 'and we can't have that, can we?'

'Auntie, before we go … what colour eyes has William got?'

'Blue eyes, the brightest blue.' Meredith gave a sudden shout of laughter, and grabbing Sandra's hand, they ran all the way to the car.

Sandra returned home to an empty house. Inside the front gate lay Prue's bicycle, front wheel buckled, handlebars askew. She let herself in with her key. No one was home. Almost dark, so where was everyone? No note on the kitchen bench. Without thinking why, she went from room to room, nervously aware of the silence.

50

Just then, her father drove up, braking hard, scraping a wheel against the kerb. He flung open the gate and hurried inside. 'Sandy?' he called. 'Quick, quick, we're going to the hospital. Prue's come off her bike, your mother's with her... I didn't want you to be home by yourself for hours.'

'What's wrong?' Sandra held her breath, not wanting to hear the answer. That twisted bicycle frightened her.

'I only know she fell off her bike on a busy road.' He drove fast, surprising Sandra by weaving in and out of the traffic, until they reached the hospital.

In the emergency ward, Prue lay propped up in bed, her arm in a sling. A raw graze covered one cheek, one eye almost closed with a swelling bruise.

Angela's face was lined with concern. '—As if we haven't enough to worry about,' she said. 'We've told you not to ride your bike on busy roads. Why can't you—'

Prue gave a little shake of her head, lips pressed together.

'When you go crashing into a fence so you don't get run over, it's most certainly a busy road.'

'Is that what happened?' Sandra looked closely at Prue's face. Tiny beads of blood seeped from the graze; her eyes were red from crying. Neither of them had ever had a bad fall, in all their years of riding bikes on rough bush roads – a few skinned knees and elbows: gravel rashes that stung in the bath.

'She dodged a car, bounced onto the footpath and hit a brick wall,' Angela explained.

Don pulled a chair alongside the bed. 'We've got to be thankful, Angela. She's a lucky girl to only get a bunged-up arm out of it. It was good of the driver to collect you and bring you both here.'

'We're still waiting for the doctor,' Angela said. 'Look at her face... what if she's broken her jaw?'

A nurse in starched cap and apron rustled in with a steel tray of clinking instruments and bandages. Prue cried miserably while her grazed cheek was cleaned and disinfected. 'There, there, it's not that bad. Be a big girl for me,' the nurse said, as she made sure there was no grit left in the wound. Although an x-ray showed her jaw wasn't broken, it hurt to open her mouth so she drank a cup of orange juice through a straw while her fractured wrist was encased in plaster.

As they drove home, quietly now, with Prue safely tucked under the car rug, Angela was still cross. 'I don't know how many times—'

'We won't go into it now, Angela.' Don said, eyes steadfastly looking ahead. 'Prue knows she did a silly thing.' He glanced in the rear-vision mirror. 'Isn't that right, Prudy?'

'What about the bike?' Sandra asked. 'Can it be fixed?'

Angela sounded upset. 'Prue certainly won't need her bicycle for quite some time. Good heavens, to think she might've been run over.'

'I'll sign my name on your plaster,' Sandra said. 'You can collect kids' signatures at school.'

Prue tried to smile, a lop-sided twitch.

23 Tyrell St, Randwick.
Saturday, 1st. July.

Dear Emmy,
An awful thing happened today, after I got home from being out with Auntie, Dad came and got me to go to the hospital because Prue had nearly been hit by a car and fell off her bike and hit a brick wall. She broke her wrist and her face looks awful with an ugly big graze and a black eye. Mum was really cross about it and Prue's bike is wrecked. I

wrote my name on her plaster cast. She's O.K. but has to drink soup through a straw until she can properly open her mouth. That's good, she can't be cheeky to me now ha ha. If Prue had got run over I'd be an only child.

That's all, I just wanted to tell you.

Love from Sandra XOX

P.S. Please call me Sandra when you write next time.

Prue went to bed early. She lay on her back, her wounded cheek covered with a gauze dressing. Her eyes were closed.

'Prue?' It was a whisper. Sandra moved closer to the bed. Light angled through the doorway from the hall. She could see that her sister was asleep, each breath a small rise and fall of the blankets.

It reminded Sandra of her visits to see Nick in hospital, his bruised face as he lay in bed, unaware of her presence. Angus might have told his mother, I'll be home for tea. How quickly people can die … one minute they're riding their bicycle, and the next … What if she'd not got out of the way and been hit by that car? Impossible to imagine. She was sorry she'd written a wicked thing to Emilia about being an only child. Emmy would never say anything so unkind. But it was too late to take it back – she'd posted the letter.

"Ferrari's Farm"
15 Bentley St., Curradeen.
9 / 7 /61.

Dear Sandra,

Poor Prue, she is lucky she only hit a wall, she must have got in big trouble for being naughty. I'm sorry she got hurt and might have got killed. It's not nice to say things like being an only child, you will have to be nice to her though I know she annoys you like my brothers do.

53

Thank you for the beautiful camisole, the creamy colour is nice and it fits me. It must have cost a lot. I had parties when I was little but Mamma says when I turn sixteen we will have a huge party with miles of cakes and spumante.

Warwick asked me to the pictures, but Pa said I couldn't go because I'm too young. I told him I'm 15 but he still said NO! I'm old enough to work in the shop but not go to the pictures with Warwick. Boo hoo.

Now that Lofty is "Warwick", I should be "Emilia". Emmy sounds baby, like you don't want to be called Sandy.

I studied real hard for the exams. In 3rd term if I don't pass every exam in the Intermediate Pa said I will have to leave school. I'm sorry your unhappy, its hard to make new friends but the girls in your class will like you better if you say hullo and smile. I bet you do good in your music exam.

I have to go now.

Love from Emilia xxxOOO

𝒴

Sandra lifted her hands from the keyboard, satisfied it was her last piece for the lesson. Without a word, Mister L'estrange presented the envelope with her exam results. His expression didn't change as she withdrew the papers and read the comments. An adequate result – not as good as with Miss Brooks, but good enough, she thought. Then without saying anything, he left her and went out to the kitchen.

She fidgeted uncomfortably. She must have read the maker's name on the piano lid a hundred times. Why was he taking so long to do whatever he was doing? Hurry up, she thought, tapping a foot on the pedal, running fingers over an arpeggio until Mister L'estrange called, 'Don't.' Then as if he relented, she heard him say, 'Play the John Field piece. Not too slowly.' Reluctantly and still impatiently, she played it.

Mister L'estrange appeared in the doorway, a tea tray in his hands. 'Leave that now, and come,' he said.

In the next room he placed the tray on a small table, indicating that she should sit in one of the armchairs. Bossy boots ... her lesson was over, so what's this? She ought to be going home – she was always the last student.

'We're having tea to finish,' he told her, 'because you know nothing of what you should know.'

What? Sandra wondered if her piano teacher had been reading *Alice in Wonderland*, to say such an odd thing. He poured tea into each wide cup from a blue china pot, a golden liquid that sent a spiral of steam towards the ceiling in the still air.

'It's best with no milk or sugar.' Mister L'estrange put a cup to his lips, took a sip. 'Fine Ceylon tea,' he said, as if to explain, and Sandra felt obliged to mimic his sips from her own cup.

'If you insist, you may have milk and sugar.' He raised an eyebrow at her across his suspended cup, 'but it's best without.'

The tea was very hot, almost impossible to drink. She would have liked to add milk and sugar, and feigned another sip, taking the opportunity to glance around the room that she only ever glimpsed from the doorway. In one corner was a fireplace; above the mantelpiece hung a vivid picture painted in dabs of blue and yellow. Several shelves were jammed with books, a sofa with a small lamp of angular pink glass fixed above it on the wall.

Mister L'estrange saw her looking. 'A slipper lamp. Each glass shade is moulded to fit only one style of frame. I like the concept.' He paused, then asked, 'do you like it?'

Taken aback, Sandra stuttered an ambivalent reply. 'I've never seen a lamp like that. Yes, I suppose so.'

'Art Deco. There are many buildings in Sydney of this era, many decorations. The more you look, the more you see, as it is with everything, hmm?'

Her tea was cooler and Sandra drank a little. Golden in its cup, oddly refreshing.

'I know something of your life from speaking to your mother,' Mister L'estrange said.

Speaking to my mother, Sandra almost yelped. When did he do that and what did she say?

'I spoke to your mother on two occasions.' He swept back his perpetually errant strand of black hair. 'The first, when she interviewed me on your headmistress's recommendation to be your piano teacher, and again a week ago, so she would know of your progress. Or not.'

Sandra didn't like the way he added that, 'Or not'. She waited for more comment, prepared for it to be unpleasant, but he had made afternoon tea, so maybe...

Suddenly he jumped to his feet. 'I forgot the biscuits.' He returned to the room with a plate. 'Macaroons. I made them myself. It isn't difficult. Egg white, almonds, sugar.'

Sandra suppressed a smile. She'd never heard of a man cooking biscuits. The macaroon crumbled at first bite and with a giggle, she sprayed crumbs into her cup of tea.

Mister L'estrange laughed – the first time Sandra had ever heard him laugh – and she was relieved not to feel her usual embarrassment.

'The biscuit trap,' he smiled. 'Be glad I didn't make biscuits with icing sugar that flies like snow on your breath when you try to eat.'

This was a different afternoon to her usual lessons where she sat at the keyboard and the teacher sat beside her, eyes watching like a hawk to see that her fingers did the right thing, correcting the smallest error in timing. Then, lesson over, she would say thank you and exit the door.

He took a thin cigarette from a pack, slowly lit it, then filled their cups again from the blue pot. 'As for your music,' he said, 'you need more work. Much more work. In your country town you were a big fish in a small sea – here you are now a very small fish. The competition is enormous. The competition to be good. To be the top.' He exhaled a gentle breath, an aroma of spice. 'You have no experience in eisteddfods, no piano competitions. Why not, I wonder?'

Sandra dug her toes into the carpet. She didn't want to hear this criticism, and had no answer, except to protest that eisteddfods and competitions were miles away in distant towns. Miss Brooks thought she was wonderful. Everyone did. Nick and his mother wanted her to play especially for them and she would have too, except Nick nearly died. Mister L'estrange was being very mean. Miss Brooks was older, she would know better. But she stayed silent, chewing her lip.

'Mozart's sonata that gets up your nose because you can't play it well enough. Oh yes—' he held up his hand to stop her automatic objection. 'The Handel in G minor, the *Gigue*… you think it's all fiddle-dee-dee, I can see it on your face. Your heart is not there. I feel it in your playing. What do you want? Unless you master technique you will be nothing.'

'I know that,' Sandra tried, now close to tears. 'But I did all right in my exams, didn't I?'

'Listen to me,' Mister L'estrange said. '*All right* is not good enough. I say this because I think you need a little shock to wake up. You're cruising. You cruise at school too, I think.'

She couldn't utter a word – she wished his fancy lamp would fall on his head and it would serve him right. Miss Brooks would never have spoken to her like that. Then it burst out of her mouth without warning. 'What do you know about me!' It was almost a cry. 'You don't know anything. You're just a ... a stupid gypsy who knows nothing at all!'

The room was thick with silence after this outburst. Mister L'estrange stubbed out his cigarette, took up the tray with both cups and pot and left the room.

Sandra could only sit in the chair, trying to stop her sniffles, stop the hurt tears. It wasn't only what her piano teacher said, but all the hurt throughout the year this far. Not simply leaving the town where she'd grown up ... her terrible yearning for the impossibility of Nick's friendship; the horrible fight with Emilia. There was the rupture in her relationship with Prue, who hardly spoke to her any more; Angela's relentless instructions every day like clockwork. Her father silent, as he went about the business of settling into his new position, his golf abandoned, with only the Easter Show and two outings to the pictures.

She wept and couldn't stop. No Emmy. Girls at school who didn't care what she thought or liked, who went to the beach in summer and what they did in winter was an unknown because only Carol spoke to her. And now even her piano teacher said horrible things.

In the midst of her unhappiness she heard the piano. As the music seeped into her, she gradually became carried away from her tears by the melody: the insistent bass, hesitations in phrasing that caused her chest to tighten with suspense. She crept to the door to listen.

Mister L'estrange played quite slowly, finally to the end. He swivelled on his seat to look at her, where she stood as if glued to the architrave.

'I, too, once wanted to be the best. One day I'll play for you more music you have never heard. It's not only classical music that I love.'

His mouth turned in a half smile. 'You called me a gypsy... perhaps you're more correct than you realize. I grew up in England, but my mother was French, from Provence. Before the war, her family moved to London where she met my father, an engineer. She was a singer. So, perhaps?'

Sandra remained at the door, downcast but listening.

'I was sent to the Sorbonne for a year – my mother said, to perfect my provincial French accent, which a Parisian could never understand. I qualified for my professional diploma in London at the Royal Academy of Music, many years of study... composition, pianoforte. I taught in Paris for several years before I came to Australia two years ago, by myself. Me and my piano. My beautiful Feurich.'

He stopped speaking. Sandra found that somehow she had gravitated to his usual stool beside her at the keyboard but now their positions were reversed. His profile as he looked down at the keyboard was fine, with straight nose, and his skin fine too; pale, closely shaven. This near, he smelled of something other than the cigarette, a delicate scent that sometimes she'd detected during lessons.

He pushed back his seat. 'You might like to wash your face before you go home, or your mother will think I've beaten you with a stick.'

'You have, sort of,' Sandra said. 'I never meant to cry, but what you said—'

'You had to be woken up. But also, now you know something of me, hmm?' He looked amused. 'Gypsy!'

In the bathroom, all creamy tiles with black and cream sunburst border atop, the face that stared at her from the mirror was patched with pink. Ugly. What was the point of all that: a lecture, a cup of tea and a recital. And now she was supposed to feel normal again?

She turned on the tap, splashed cold water onto her cheeks, and while drying her face on what looked like a spare towel, she glanced around. On a porcelain shelf stood an array of brushes and bottles. One small bottle was conspicuous: clear glass, squat, with a glass stopper on which sat the shape of a small dog – she thought it a rather ugly little dog. She peered closer and saw a name inscribed on the glass: Toujours fidèle. Certainly Mister L'estrange sometimes smelled different. But perfume?

She closed the bathroom door behind her. She would need to find another occasion to visit the bathroom for a thorough investigation.

> *23 Tyrell St, Randwick.*
> *18/ 7 /61.*

Dear Emilia,

Mr. L'estrange was so nasty to me at my lesson today. He said I should have done better in my exam and I'm lazy at school too! He told me I play Mozart like it gets up my nose and I'll never be any good if I don't work harder. I got so upset that I cried.

He made a cup of tea and later he played a beautiful piece on the piano so maybe he's half right because I haven't felt like playing since I got here. Mum likes him because I can walk to his flat for lessons and she never mentions his earring. She says the way I talk about Aunt Meredith it sounds like I would rather live with her than my family. Maybe I'll go and live with Auntie and that will serve Mum right.

Prue's sore cheek is still very pink. She hardly ever speaks to me, she's always with her best friend who lives down the road, lucky thing. It's NOT FAIR. And now Prue is taller than me. I hate her.

The only nice thing this week was Dad bought a new stereo record player, because ours got broken when we moved.

With love from your desperate friend
Sandra XXXXXXX

"Ferrari's Farm."
15 Bentley St., Curradeen.
24/ 7 /61.

Dear Sandra,

Your piano teacher sounds real mean. I told Mamma about him and afternoon tea after your lesson and she said be careful because your 15 and growing up and something might happen because some men can't help themselves. I'm not sure what she means by that because he is your teacher. Are you really going to live with your auntie? She sounds nice.

You shouldn't hate Prue, she's lucky to have a best friend down the road. My mother says it's jealousy when someone else has what you want. I wish you still lived here, I go to the roller skate rink but it's not the same without you. Remember one day we laughed so much we nearly wet ourselves? Some kids ride on the footpaths but I'm scared I'll fall off.

I got good marks in my exams, I nearly died of shock. Nonna showed me how to knit a bolero with real thin wool and it will look good.

I'll write more next time. Lucky you to have a record player, we don't.

Love from your best friend forever
Emilia xxx

Afraid to close her eyes, afraid another bad dream might invade her sleep, each night Sandra lay awake and restless. Before her performance in the Curradeen concert last year, she'd dreamed the piano wouldn't play and peering inside she discovered there were no hammers or strings: the piano was empty. A wave of discontent spread throughout the hall and terrified, she'd fled from the stage before the storm erupted.

Sleepless, she watched the moonlight slipping across her window. Mister L'estrange had called her a very small fish. 'The competition is enormous.' he'd said, and then he'd cut her down with his next words, 'You have no experience in eisteddfods, no piano competitions.' It was true ... Miss Brooks had never pushed her in that direction – eisteddfods and competitions were always in distant towns. Was that so terrible? Eisteddfods? Phooey.

Closing her eyes, she relived the real and beautiful evening in the Curradeen town hall: again she heard the applause for her *Clair de Lune*, Nick's mother congratulating her, his brief kiss on her cheek, family and friends, and dear Miss Brooks. Home by midnight, she'd placed her bouquet of carnations on the piano, once more played *Clair de Lune* ... she had been happier as a big fish in a small sea.

Unrelenting, a dream quietly possessed her ... in a huge hall, she saw thousands of blank upturned faces crowded and staring; heard the rustle of their impatience. Seated at a grand piano, her fingers slipped on the keys, striking discordant notes. In her dream, she heard a voice shout – muffled and indistinct as she strained to hear. Scraps of paper blew into her face, carpeting the floor ... the piano lifted on the wind, rocked and settled. Again she heard the wordless voice. In the vast expanse of the hall she sat by herself – no one had stayed to hear her play.

Suddenly awake, wide-eyed, she lay still as remnants of the dream flickered and faded. The truth eclipsed any uncertainty: she no longer wanted to be the famous concert pianist she'd always pictured – the attentive applause from an adoring public, the fuss and flowers. Of course it wasn't like that. It meant years of back-breaking hard work with a tiny percentage of winners.

No, it was simply music she wanted – to immerse herself in her own songs, the songs she made up. She didn't need the Conservatorium High School, only needed a good teacher. Mister L'estrange? His voice in the dream...

Her feet were freezing. The hot water bottle had gone cold and she kicked it away. The luminous clock showed four a.m. She crawled out of bed, found her eiderdown from where it had slipped onto the floor... why hadn't she worn bed socks... Please Mum, buy me an electric blanket.

Snuggled under blankets and eiderdown, Sandra felt Ginger's careful paws treading along her bed, the weight of his body as the cat settled heavily beside her. Nothing of the dream remained and she felt strangely relaxed, comforted by the warmth of the old cat.

'Dear old Ginge, have you come to keep me company?' She stroked his head, felt a purr vibrate beneath her hand. 'Guess what,' she whispered into his fur, 'I'll still learn piano, but I'm going to write my own songs too, exactly how I like, and too bad what anyone says. But that's our secret, so you mustn't tell.'

His fur tickled her nose and she pulled up the blanket. 'You should have a song all of your own, Ginger. What do you think? Tomorrow we'll make one up, maybe a little cat dance...'

five.

Afternoon tea at the kitchen table no longer included Don, quietly packing tobacco into his pipe, Ginger invariably sitting at his feet, while Angela beat egg flips for Sandra and Prue, then poured the tea and asked questions about school.

These days, Don had afternoon tea in the staffroom at the bank. Angela made sure she was home by 3.30, unlike in Curradeen when she might be at a CWA or Red Cross meeting. Back then, it had been normal for Sandra and Prue to cycle home after school, amuse themselves alone. But Sydney's eastern suburbs still reverberated with the kidnapping and murder of a small boy last year.

Angela put a large plate on the table. 'I've made neenish tarts today. It's a treat because considering it's a new school, you both did quite well in your exams.'

Prue immediately chose a tart and bit into it: 'Gee Mum, the best tart you ever made,' she said through a mouthful of mock cream and raspberry jam.

Sandra reached for a tart, her hand momentarily poised in mid-air with Angela's next remark:

'Maths and science seem to be your weak point, Sandy. Maybe by the end of the year you'll have caught up and it won't seem so strange.' She poured herself a cup of tea, pleased at how her tarts were disappearing.

'I hate both those subjects,' Sandra replied, licking cream off her fingers. 'And *pleeease* don't keep calling me *Sandy*.'

'Perhaps we can find you a coach for after school.'

'I don't want a coach.'

'Then maybe you can put in some extra time at the weekend. A few less outings with Aunt Meredith, perhaps.'

'You go out all day looking at flower shops. We only go out on Saturday mornings and I'm always home in time to practise.' Sandra put her glass down heavily, slopping milk onto the table.

'Oh dear, hurry and get the dishcloth. What do you and Aunt Meredith do on all these outings?'

'We just go around the shops, or into town or … I don't know, just *around*.'

'I might have a word to her—'

'That's not fair,' Sandra angrily dumped the dishcloth into the sink. How could her mother think of taking away those wonderful opportunities with Aunt Meredith, their shopping excursions, Auntie's never-ending story.

The neenish plate was empty and Angela pushed back her chair. 'We'll talk about it over the weekend,' she announced. 'I'll see what your father thinks.'

'Dad will know exactly how I feel,' Sandra objected. 'Coaching will be awful. It won't do any good. I hate science and especially chemistry—'

Angela interrupted, 'By the time you leave school you should have a well-rounded education, and have—'

'Mum, you sound like a text book! What does school teach that you can't learn by reading books at home? I don't like my teachers – except for English, she's nice.'

'That's enough. We'll discuss it after I've talked to your father. And I might go and see your piano teacher too.'

Sandra heard a snigger from Prue and scowled at her. 'Go jump in the lake, prune face,' she hissed at Prue's retreating back. Perhaps she should've revealed her secret, right then: dropped a bombshell right into the middle of the neenish tarts and her mother's lecture.

Ginger was curled on an armchair, audibly purring. It looked such a comfortable scene, except for those ominous words. Angela had diplomatically taken Prue to the pictures – that was something different for a Saturday. No florist shops today.

With a glance at Sandra, Don tapped out his pipe on the ashtray, opened his tin of tobacco. 'Your mother's concerned that your school marks aren't what they should be.'

Sandra already felt uneasy. 'It's just because I'm new.'

'Halfway through the year, my dear, time to pull your socks up. Your mother suggests a coach for maths and science, perhaps on Saturday mornings.'

'Dad, I'm not interested in those subjects. I get enough maths out of my music. It's not all just counting … scales have numerical ratios. Patterns and rhythms follow mathematical laws, and contrapuntal compositions like Bach's fugues—'

'You can't possibly compare the two.'

'Just give me a bit more time. I'll work harder, Dad, I promise.'

'We've heard this before. No, your mother's right. I think for the time being you'll have to stay home on Saturdays and we'll find a coach.' He held up a finger as Sandra was about to object. 'Meredith will understand – she knows the benefit of having solid foundations.'

'It won't make any difference. I hate school. I hate it hate it *hate it*!'

Before her tears fell, Sandra fled from the lounge room, banging the bedroom door behind her. They don't understand, they never did and they never will, she wept. Snatching the hairbrush, she struck hard across her knuckles, saw with angry satisfaction how bluish lumps instantly rose on each one, then flinging herself down on the bed, she buried her face in the pillow. All this, and Mister L'estrange telling me off... Everything was going wrong – why couldn't she be happy?

Tears dried, she rolled over to stare at the ceiling. Maybe she was mistaken that the family had settled? Her father often got home late, tired and irritable, and no florist had offered her mother a job. How come Prue behaved as if nothing worried her, ever? Friends had scribbled their names all over her plaster cast and she carried it like a trophy, often weaving through the house singing *That'll be the Day,* or copying Buddy Holly's Pe-hh-ggy Sue Pe-hh-ggy Sue. It was enough to make you puke.

She turned to face the wall, pushing her bruised fingers under the pillow. At least when she played the piano, the keyboard became her real world: seated at the piano she was always a princess. And now Mister L'estrange was threatening that. Wait till I tell them all I won't audition for the con... She sighed at the thought – there'll be another big row.

Nick was so far away. If only she could see him again... and again and again. Why didn't her mother tell her she'd written to Mrs Morgan ages ago? Their meeting in Curradeen's main street had been so brief, like lightning, and then he was walking away with his mother to catch a plane.

Maybe that was her fate. She would always be saying goodbye to Nick: his kiss after the Apex concert last year, and again after their day out in Sydney – the magic spot on her forehead that almost made her faint; her midnight kiss in hospital as Nick lay unconscious, and lastly in Curradeen when she'd kissed his cheek, touched his skin, felt his warmth. Gone gone gone. Deep inside, she felt only a vast emptiness.

Fresh tears gathered in the corners of her eyes and she swung her legs onto the floor, ran fingers through her tousled hair, then savagely brushed it, twisting a band around a rough ponytail. Sleeves pushed up she saw the tiny, faint scar on her forearm where she'd jabbed the scissors that terrible day of Nick's accident. The wound had achieved nothing, except to camouflage her frightful, helpless despair and horrify her family. Crumpled on the floor, her father had held her weeping body in his arms, unable to speak except to repeat, 'It's all right, it's all right, ssssh.'

She stared at her reflection. The face in the mirror looked haunted. She felt the pulse beating in her neck and ran a finger down the place where she knew the artery to be. Her veins were blue beneath the skin. She remembered as a small child how she'd sat alone under a tree in the garden, felt the blood beat in her wrists and for the first time wondered if she was living inside a dream, and if she were to wake up, would she still exist? No, this definitely wasn't a dream.

At dinner on their first night in Randwick, Aunt Meredith had declared, 'Life is full of variables ...' and how our paths criss-crossed, and 'make of it what you will.' Perhaps this is what she meant: Sandra was the only one who could figure out what to do and which way to go, on both her real and imaginary pathways. Something would have to change, and she was the only one who could make that change.

Later, almost dark with a chill wind beginning to blow, the house quiet for hours, Sandra's bedroom door stayed firmly shut and Don immersed in the Saturday business papers. The week had been busy, too many customers complaining and begging.

The front door slammed on a wintry draught as Angela and Prue returned home. 'We saw a cowboy film,' Prue told her father.

'Mum didn't like it but I did. It was so exciting with Red Indians creeping up on the cowboys sitting around a campfire, and suddenly—'

Angela stopped her mid-sentence. 'That'll do, dear. Go and wash your hands and you can help me get dinner.' She waited until Prue darted from the lounge room, then asked, 'How did your talk go?'

'Well, not good … she was very upset. She shouted at me how she hated school. I haven't spoken to Meredith yet … maybe we should leave it for a while.'

'Not now we've set the ball rolling. There'll be advertisements for coaches in the local paper, though I've no idea how much they charge. Did she do her practice?'

'Not a sound since she slammed her bedroom door.'

'Sulking won't do,' Angela said. 'I'll see what she's up to.'

She was back in a moment. 'Her room's empty. Didn't you hear her go out?'

'No, she's been quiet as a mouse since our talk.'

'She's sneaked out somehow,' Angela's voice developed an anxious edge. 'Don't tell me she's run away again.'

Meredith didn't look happy to open her front door and find Sandra on the doorstep. 'Sandra! Good heavens, you surely didn't walk here. It's nearly dark, did you get a bus?'

Sandra was close to tears. 'Bus. And then I walked.'

'You're frozen. Do your mother and father know where you are? No, I don't suppose they do.'

As she rubbed Sandra's cold fingers, Meredith drew in a shocked breath. 'What's this? You've hurt yourself.'

'It's nothing. We had a row and I whacked it, that's all. I said I hated school … but I don't really, I'm just sick of it.'

Together on the couch, Sandra huddled into her aunt's shoulder, eyes closed to block the image of her parents' stern faces. Oh, the comfort of holding Auntie's hand, so different, she thought, from last year when I sat here and told her about Nick, and she treated me like a grown-up and everything was wonderful.

'Mum and Dad want me to have maths and science coaching and not go out with you anymore.'

'Aah.' A fleeting shadow crossed Meredith's face. 'Is it so serious? You've left behind everything that was familiar, your best friend Emilia and Nick. It looked like a lovely friendship would develop, when puff! all of a sudden it all vanished. I'm sure that's very hard for you.'

Sandra sat quietly, listening to her aunt's gentle voice. Although she could be noisy with chatter and loud laughter, Meredith's home always had a calming effect. Like a refuge protected by the lovely surroundings: reflections on polished floors, the colours and textures; flowers hanging over the courtyard trellis. Meredith might play her piano or a record from the vast collection of LPs. Dear Auntie, always so ready to listen. Yes – Sandra allowed herself to sink into the velvet cushion – it's my refuge.

'We love so deeply at your age,' Meredith consoled. 'It's our first love, and whatever may follow, we never forget it.'

'After Nick's accident, Emilia told Mum I loved Nick, but she didn't believe it. She said he's too old for me.'

'I'm sure your mother understood your deep affection for him.'

Sandra was determined not to weep. Be strong, she told herself. Be strong. 'There's only five years' difference. And I *love* Nick!'

'I know you do. It's going to take time for you to accommodate this change. The whole world is waiting for you, especially your music. But you need to do well at school, too.' She lifted Sandra's hand to her lips, kissed the hurt little fingers, caressed her cheek. 'Better now?'

Fetching a brush, Meredith released Sandra's tangled ponytail from its band, gently stroked it smooth. 'It isn't good to run away like that, a pretty girl alone in the street at night.' She slipped her shoes on. 'Come along, I'll drive you home, the family will be worried. What on earth is Angela going to say!'

Tyrell St, Randwick.
30/ 7 /61.

Dear Emilia,

I had a big argument with Mum and all because I said I hated school and I can't help that, can I? I want to do something more than sit in a stuffy classroom. Mum started off being nice and making a special afternoon tea but then I got a lecture. Yesterday Dad told me I've got to have coaching and not go out with Auntie any more. I went to Auntie's place but she said I was wrong to run away and took me home. Nobody understands how I feel.

My marks for English, History and Geography were all over 70% but I only just passed Maths and Science, I don't much like chemistry, I got 55% !! Phooey to that. What's the use of chemistry when I leave school and only want to write songs. I don't want to be a concert pianist any more but you can't tell anyone. And worse, I don't want to go to the Conservatorium High School next year, but I'm scared to say anything because Mum will be so cross.

Love from your desperate friend
Sandra XOX

Dear Sandra,

That's real crook, what you told me. Can't you get your auntie to stick up for you? Mamma says your mum and dad are right, but.

Coaches cost a lot of money so maybe you won't have to. Why don't you want to go to the conservatrium high school any more, it's all you use to talk about.

Roger asked me to go to the pictures on Saturday, I really want to see Debbie Reynolds in "Tammy" but I'm not going. I'd rather go with Warwick, but Pa won't let me anyway so it was easy to say I'm not allowed.

In English class Miss Pearce went on and on about an American man called Hemmingway who shot hisself, how can anyone do such a horrible thing, his poor family. She said he wrote lots of books but I never heard of him.

I made my bolero and it fits me! Nonna says it's beautiful and I think so too. The colour is green and I didn't make any mistakes. I can wear it to the pictures if I ever get to go with Warwick. He has got so tall now you would be surprised.

Cheer up. I will write more next time.

Love from Emilia XXX

23 Tyrell St., Randwick,
13 / 8 / 61.

Dearest Emilia,

Yippee, I don't have to have a coach. Dad said I've got another chance. It might be too expensive, like you said and Mum didn't say anything more either.

I can't tell them yet about the Con High School, there'll only be another argument. I know I talked about it lots, but I've changed my mind. I'll never work hard enough or practice long enough, the audition will be awful and I'd have to prove I <u>really really</u> want to be accepted. I would just die.

Now I'm going better with Mr. L as my teacher so why change schools?

Your bolero sounds pretty. I've never tried to knit but Prue learned last summer. She's gone crazy on rock and roll singers and her bedroom wall is plastered in cut outs. Her bike is still in the shed with mine and Dad isn't fixing it yet.

We've been here 9 months. Our house looks really good now and Mum is growing a flower garden with all her favourites. She asked if your father can please send her some zookeenie seeds and also tell her how to grow them?

I looked up "Warwick" in my book of names, it's Anglo-Saxon and the first ones lived in Warwickshire and were Lords of the Manor in 1050 !!!

I've heard of Ernest Hemingway, there is a book in the school library but I never read it. Nobody should be so sad they commit suicide, I can't imagine it.

Have you seen Nick or his mother again? More news please.

Remember it's a secret what I told you about the Con high school.

Love from Sandra xox

"Ferrari's Farm," Curradeen.
18 / 8 / 61.

Dear Sandra,

It's good your happy again, but you have to tell them about the Con soon. Fingers crossed you don't get into big trouble. I promise I won't say anything about your secret.

I told Warwick about his name and he already knows. Nobody has got used to calling him that so he is still called Lofty.

No, I never saw Nick or his mother since your visit. We had a big frost this morning and Pa got angry because some of his vegies went all black. I will ask him about the seeds for your mother.

Some girls in my class walk around knitting at recess with a ball of wool stuck under their arm. I'm going to try it at home when no one's looking. There are some of us want to start a "Marching Girls" team! I am real excited to think about it and we can make up our uniforms.

Love from Emilia XOX

Six.

Life settled, little by little, into a routine. Once again, Don told the family stories from his days at the bank – so different to those from Curradeen, such as the farmer who dreamed of a fish farm. Angela gave up searching the classifieds for a job, 'At least for a while,' she decided. 'Perhaps I should learn cake decorating instead of hoping for a florist shop,' and the kitchen drawers became tangled with cutters, crimpers and innumerable sized piping tubes.

Prue managed to finish knitting a sweater – thick wool and thicker needles, and although one sleeve seemed a trifle longer than the other, she was proud of it. Sandra deliberately ignored her sister's expeditions to the Stadium, and Prue left Sandra alone.

No one referred to the subject of a maths coach again and Sandra practised her study pieces diligently, making no attempt to reveal her secret decision not to audition, even to Meredith. She was more contented than she'd felt for months. What was the use, she mused, of wishing and wishing, for what had gone forever.

But in the midst of her unfamiliar contentment, she worried that too much time was slipping by since she'd asked Aunt Meredith about the photograph, and she was afraid her aunt would forget to tell her more about William. A bus trip to Bronte next Saturday was needed, for her to solve the mystery.

Meredith was busy in the kitchen when Sandra knocked on her door. She dried cups on a tea towel, brewed tea, and they sat in the sheltered courtyard.

'William built the trellis so I could grow a climbing rose,' Meredith said, pouring tea into each cup. 'I love how it goes mad with flowers in spring and autumn – huge floppy pink roses with a divine scent. Another few weeks and you'll see it covered in flowers.'

'My piano teacher makes afternoon tea after my lessons,' Sandra volunteered. 'It's Ceylon tea and I've got used to drinking it without milk or sugar.'

'Really?' Meredith's eyebrows shot up. 'Then your lessons have become somewhat extended. I hope you're making progress amidst these cups of tea. You must like your teacher now … I remember at the start, you couldn't stand him. Isn't that so?'

'Yes, but I've learned such a lot, not just my piano studies, but other things too. He's like nobody I've ever met before.'

'And I wonder what that could mean. Does your mother know?'

'Oh Auntie, no. She'd make all sorts of objections. I can't believe I hated him before, because he's very polite and he's got lots to talk about. He told me about this magic place in the south of France with wild white horses, where the river runs into the sea, and there's a castle in Spain hundreds of years old that's got beautiful Persian gardens and a fountain with twelve marble lions, I can't remember the name. And he always plays a piece before I leave.'

'I expect it's all right, Angela tells me he's a good teacher, regardless of his earring which I've heard about.' Meredith tipped the teapot to refill their cups.

William's story was taking forever, Sandra anguished. If only she doesn't get up now to choose a record. 'The photograph, Auntie …' she cajoled her. 'William is so handsome – you have to tell me more. Why does it say "Austinmer" on the back, and what happened after you ran away together?'

'All these questions ... you're a determined girl aren't you? I hope you work that hard at school – you should be in a debating team.'

'You got up to where his family died in a plane crash. Did they ever find out what happened?'

'Ah, that dreadful day,' Meredith sighed. 'His father radioed that a fog had come down, he'd lost visibility. The plane's wheels must've got caught in treetops – a miscalculation I suppose – the wreckage was scattered about and difficult to find in rough country.'

'Oh, he lost all his family at once. Poor William.'

'Yes, poor William, but we still had each other ... and he'd inherited the family home, all the properties. Overnight he became a very wealthy young man – a young man with no career except two years in the army and a girlfriend who'd just left school!'

'So what did you do?'

'Will got jobs here and there. He'd resisted his father's attempts to train him in business, but he was clever and handsome, with a silver tongue – he could wind people around his little finger. Rationing continued for some time after the war, and Will used his contacts to get various things for us, especially dress materials so I could sew my own clothes, and dresses for my girlfriends.'

'Didn't your parents try to make you come home?'

'William had plenty of money. They couldn't force me to return home. For several years, I didn't see my family. Donald sometimes phoned. I was invited to your parents' wedding, but not William, so I didn't go.'

'That's sad. No wonder Mum and Dad never used to talk about you.'

'It's mended now,' Meredith said. 'Our parents are long dead. We always avoided any reference to it when you came for holidays. And we all have a nice time together now, don't we?'

Sandra thought it was an odd question. But Aunt Meredith always spoke to her as an adult, so why not? 'Yes, and I'm glad.' She hesitated, then said carefully, 'But I don't think you've told me all about William yet.'

'The worst story is yet to come, but I've had enough today. It's a big thing, to dredge all this history up, the emotion it brings – but somehow it feels good to tell you, and perhaps it might help you, too.'

Meredith stretched her arms up, straightening her back. 'Come inside and we'll play some music. There's a new shop in Rowe Street, the most wonderful records – we should go there one day.'

Deep in her heart, Sandra wondered why Aunt Meredith had chosen to relate her love story. Now she had an inkling of the very dark secret behind Meredith's veneer of glamour and good humour. But why tell her? Yes, there was a similarity between fifteen-year-old Meredith's love for William and her own feelings for Nick. Auntie knew how she loved him, but there had been nothing further. Nick never realized how she adored him although they'd breezily wandered the city together that special day, whereas Aunt Meredith ran away with her true love. So where was William now? Her final words in the story had been, The worst is yet to come.

9

Frankie Laine sang the *Rawhide* theme song as Randy Yates and the boys cantered into the black and white distance. Don turned off the TV and settled into reading the newspaper; Angela picked up her book to continue studying English gardens. Prue was curled into her armchair with Ginger as if she'd like to stay there for the night.

Her feet resting on a pouffe, Sandra occupied half the couch with her mother. This was the chance she'd been anticipating. 'I've *decided…*' she said with emphasis, pausing for effect to be sure she had her parents' attention, 'I've decided that I don't want to go to the Conservatorium High School.'

Silence continued for a moment, then Angela exclaimed, 'What? What on earth are you talking about?'

'I'm doing well learning with Mister L'estrange. I know you think he's *common* because you don't like his earring, but that doesn't make him a bad teacher.'

Don put down his paper. 'This is contrary to everything you worked towards with Miss Brooks,' he frowned. 'You've always been passionate about going to the Conservatorium High School as a stepping stone to university. Why have you suddenly changed your mind?'

Sandra refused to look past her toes in their woollen socks, concentrating on her prepared speech. 'It's very simple. I was passionate about it when I lived in Curradeen. Now I don't want to do it any more.'

'Sandra dear, think again,' Angela almost pleaded, her garden book sliding unnoticed to the floor. 'This is right out of the blue. We need to talk about it.'

'I knew you'd say that. It isn't out of the blue. I've thought about it for weeks.' She glanced at Prue, who shifted position and levered Ginger off her lap. 'And don't you say anything,' she warned her sister.

'But your audition's already arranged,' Angela said.

'We can cancel it, can't we?'

'I won't have you throw away all your work and all the money we've spent on lessons—'

'Mum! I'm not throwing anything away. This year's been horrible; the only nice thing has been going out with auntie and learning music with Mister L'estrange. He treats me properly, and I'm getting good marks at school now, so why change?'

'There you go again,' Angela said. 'Fancy saying the only nice thing has been going out with Meredith. That's a very unkind thing to say when I've always tried so hard to be helpful.'

Bemused by this turn of events, Don collected his pipe and tobacco. He dropped a kiss on Sandra's head. 'Goodnight. It's a big decision. We'll talk about it tomorrow.' And he left the room to a deeper, shocked silence.

23 Tyrell St., Randwick,
25 / 8 / 61.

Dear Emilia,

I finally told Mum and Dad last night I won't go to the Con High School. They were very cranky and said we'll talk about it tomorrow, same as always.

When Mr.L plays the piano, he's so brilliant I bet he's better than the Con teachers. I don't think I will ever be that clever. That's being REALISTIC! I haven't told him yet, I wonder what he'll say.

I'm so happy when I make up my songs so that's what I'm going to do. It's funny because Mum never notices, she must think it's all in my syllabus. The year after next is the Leaving Certificate and when I've left school I can study music at university if I want to.

I can't write any more tonight after talking to Mum and Dad. Sleep tight,
love from Sandra XOXO

"Ferrari's Farm," Curradeen.
3 / 9 / 61.

Dear Sandra,

Gee, you played so good at the concert, everyone said so. I told Mamma and she said maybe you have lost confidance. You will have to tell your piano teacher. Can you keep learning with him? It sounds like you probably thought about it all for ages and ages.

Roger followed me when I went to feed the chooks yesterday. He kissed me when I wasn't looking I got such a surprise. He's nice but I like Lofty better, he walks me home from school on days when he doesn't get the bus, except when it's holidays and he's back at the farm.

Marching girls uniforms will be real expensive but not if we make our own. There are 7 of us which makes one leader and 6 girls to march in rows. We can practice marching to records of band music and then march with the town band when our flower festival is on.

I feel very good that I can do something different to school and the shop every day. If you were here you could be in the team too and we could march together.

I'm going to talk about it tonight and they'll be surprised that's for sure.

Love from Emilia XXX

23 Tyrell St, Randwick.
11 / 9 / 61.

Dearest Emilia,

Eeek, Roger kissed you, what did it feel like? Did you kiss him back and does anyone know? It's funny because I sort of miss Lofty too, although he was annoying when he followed us around like a puppy.

I knew you would understand about the Con and everything. Your mother might be right and the thought of piano competitions frightens me to death. I'm scared to think what Mr. L will say, it was bad enough telling Mum and

Dad with Prue sitting there making faces.

I feel like I don't belong here and there's nothing I can do about it. I'm still friends with Carol but we don't talk about anything much, just school and other kids. She's had her hair straightened and it looks nice. I haven't got anything to do these hols.

Mum and Dad gave Prue a fountain pen for her 13th birthday and I gave her a Ricky Nelson record "Hello Mary-Lou." Her plaster cast is off and her skin is all wrinkly, but it's better. She sneaks off to rock and roll concerts at the Stadium on Saturday afternoons with her girlfriends. She might get into trouble with bad boys. Do you think I should tell on her?

Give me more news about Roger, what does he look like? I don't know any boys here but lots get the same bus as me. Will you really be a marching girl? I don't think I would like all that drill and marching like the army.

Love from Sandra XXX

"Ferrari's Farm,"
20 / 9 / 61.

Dear Sandra,

I got your letter. I don't know if you should tell on Prue. It's not nice to tittletat but she may get into trouble if you don't. Can you tell your auntie instead or you could go with Prue to find out what it's like?

Roger is short but he is real strong like a footy player, he has a crew cut. He works hard in Pa's vegie garden and can drive the truck but only inside our fence. He hasn't tried to kiss me again so maybe it was an experament. I don't mind as he was real nice about it. Nobody knows and you can't tell anyone!

About marching girls I haven't told Mamma and Pa yet. I want to have a white pleated skirt with a red jacket and gold buttons down each side. We can buy white peaked caps with a red and gold band around. It's going to be fun and <u>not</u> like the army and I'm really happy to find something I will love doing.

Tell me all about your piano teacher what he says next letter. He sounds real scarey!

I've sat in the shop most of the holidays.

love from Emilia XXOOXX

7

'I knew it. I knew it!' Mister L'estrange leapt to his feet, clapping his hands before spinning on his heel to fix Sandra with a gimlet eye.

Sandra watched him with amazement. At the end of her lesson, she'd taken a deep breath, steeled herself as she counted to three, and faced her music teacher. But all she managed to say was, 'I've changed my mind, I don't want to audition for the Con—' She'd hardly got the words out of her mouth and off he went. This was an entirely unexpected outcome. Anticipating a scene, she'd stuffed handkerchiefs into her pocket in case she cried. Disconcerted, she turned back to the keyboard.

Finally he came to sit beside her at the piano. She heard him exhale a long breath, and prepared herself for an accusation similar to her mother's.

'My dear girl,' he began, but gently. When she looked up quickly, he held up his hand for silence. 'I've seen this coming,' he continued. 'You play very well, very well indeed, technically you are much improved. But the heart is missing, regardless of my talk with you in July about exactly this thing.'

It was a damning comment and her heart lurched, her throat thickening as tears threatened. Mister L'estrange wasn't to be hurried; he would speak his mind and she was obliged to sit there and listen.

'Your heart may no longer be in place for performance, but your dream lies elsewhere. You are not fully aware, I think. Let me explain.'

Bracing herself to hear the rest of his condemnation, Sandra sat facing the black and white keys.

'When I'm out of the room I hear you quietly play your own pieces. You think I can't hear you, but I listen. I listen closely. You think nobody notices when you stray from the syllabus, but we know. Your mother told me you play made up songs at home?'

'She's never said—' Sandra burst out, but again Mister L'estrange held up his hand.

'Your mother's impression is that it interferes with your studies, but it's not the case. I wonder that your mother doesn't really hear—'

Sandra sighed, shoulders slumped, beginning to feel sorry she'd opened her mouth about the conservatorium. 'They're just songs I make up.'

Mister L'estrange gave a snort of laughter. 'Don't you realize you already have a repertoire of your own compositions?'

His enthusiasm surprised her, and she shook her head. 'Then what am I supposed to do?'

'Believe it or not, this is the road I think you should pursue,' he said. 'Your songs are beautiful, even strange... the harmonic patterns you make. I find your compositions almost other-worldly, mysterious. *This* is where your heart lies, yes? If this is true, then forget the conservatorium for now – there are many brilliant teachers in the world. Pass your exams at school and continue with me if you wish – I'd be happy to nurture such a beautiful talent. It's better for you, Sandra, far better, if you no longer have the fire to perform, the ambition. For some, the classroom is perfect...'

His words trailed off. 'Whatever you do, the decision must be yours.'

For several minutes he didn't speak. Sandra kept silent too, absorbing the notion that his words resonated with her deepest desire to compose. Mister L'estrange said her own pieces were beautiful.

'Have you transcribed your compositions?' he asked. 'Noted them down properly?'

Again Sandra shook her head. 'No, but I remember them all, every single one, every variation.'

'Good, good, that's an art in itself. Beethoven claimed he remembered every one of his improvisations.' His teeth flashed in a smile. 'Clever girl. But transcribe them to make sure of it. Put them on paper so you can build on what you've got. What do you think, hmm?'

She stared at him, sitting calmly on his stool. 'It's what I'd rather do,' she admitted, 'but I thought you'd be angry with me for wasting time, like my mother said.'

'You have never wasted time, Sandra. There were times you were lazy, but we've already talked about that. This is a new direction, and if you want, it's the best direction. I've felt it whenever I heard you play your own music, when you thought I couldn't hear you.' He laughed long and hard, then motioning her to move over, he positioned himself at the keyboard. 'Listen to this...'

And he played the piece that he'd played that afternoon in July when he'd scolded her severely for cruising, as he put it. The lovely melody had carried her away from her tears, the insistent bass, the hesitations in phrasing that left her breathless. She listened intently until the final note.

'It's mine,' Mister L'estrange said. 'I composed it when I was studying musicology.'

'But it's beautiful.'

'But, but? You're surprised because *I* composed it? Every piece I've played for you after our tea has been mine.'

'—I didn't mean to be rude.'

'I know that. I love to compose, and I recognize the same spirit in you. You have your own songs buzzing in your head, striving to be free. And they *will* be free... our best songs nest in our souls, waiting for the moment...

'Buy yourself a ream of blank sheet music, get the ten-stave format – note it how you hear it, so it's not forgotten.' He waved his hand, 'accidents happen, and we don't want to lose anything. And never mind, I'll speak to your parents.'

Mister L'estrange looked elated, and Sandra realized that she'd hardly breathed since he'd clapped his hands, saying, 'I knew it!'

He closed the lid of the piano, stood up to stretch, looking very satisfied. 'And now it's definitely time for a cup of tea.'

23 Tyrell St, Randwick,
27 / 9 / 61.

Dear Emilia,

Here's what happened at my lesson. When I said I didn't want to audition Mr. L told me that I play very well but if I don't have the "fire" I should give up performance and compose music instead!!! and he wasn't annoyed I don't want to go to the con high school. He said there's lots of brilliant teachers in the world, I wonder if he meant himself, hee hee?

All the pieces he's played for me after my lessons are his own compositions and I never knew. This is my "road"– that's what he said. I was so scared that he'd be angry like Mum and Dad, but he told me to go and buy a heap of blank sheets and write it all down.

That's all I can think about right now! I wish I could see

you and talk like we used to. Would you be allowed to stay
with me over Christmas hols?
love from your happy friend!
Sandra xxxxxxxxxxxxOOO

"Ferrari's Farm," Curradeen.
3rd. October, 61.

Dear Sandra,

That's really good about your piano. I bet you're excited, you were so scared it was going to be horrible. I told Mamma and she says it shows we shouldn't expect bad things to happen all the time but look for the good things in life. It's hard but, when it's exams and that.

One day maybe I'll hear you play your songs and you'll be a famous composer. I am happy for you because I know you've been sad this year.

Lofty stays in town now with his relatives so he doesn't get the bus and he walks me home every day. We are going to the roller skate rink at the weekend. He's got new glasses so he's not googly eyes any more. We were unkind calling him that but he always laughed.

I'm not allowed be a marching girl because Pa says I would show off my legs in a short skirt above my knees. How can he say that when he's never seen a marching girl team. Boo hoo.

I'll ask if I can visit, I hope so, I've never seen the sea.

Love always from Emilia XXXOOO

9

Sometimes she thought it might be his hair, the thick inky silk of it. Sometimes she wondered if it might be the glisten in his dark eyes. But mostly Sandra had grown aware, so fully aware, of Mister L'estrange's presence during her lessons: his quiet self seated next to her, intently watching, listening as she played; the scent of his skin, its smoothness, his cheek at times quite close as he leaned to point at the page. But, she thought, it's normal to be so close – he's my piano teacher – it's normal to be so conscious of him. Isn't it?

He'd offered to nurture her talent … she heard the echo of his voice, 'Your songs are beautiful and mysterious.' There persisted the odd little shiver if he accidentally touched her arm, or leaned across to demonstrate how a trill or a phrase should be played. She liked his hands, his slim wrists disappearing into shirt sleeves, or the rare times when he wore a tee-shirt snug about his torso, the muscles of his shoulders showing broad and firm.

But when he accused her of cruising and she called him a gypsy, he showed another side of himself, a different side that she thought hid a fiery core. He'd picked up the tray and stalked out of the room – disappeared to play his beautiful music, dissipate the fury, all possible anger that he might have felt – it had carried her away, suspended breath, caused her to doubt her very self.

She had to admit, it was exciting. She pictured staying until the blue teapot was dry, their cups were empty, and Mister L'estrange would suggest they sit on the sofa together. He would rest his arm along the back of the couch, play with her hair, run his fingers beneath the curve of her hair's weight, his fingers light on her neck, and he would kiss her, and she would allow herself to sink into him, allow her first sweet kiss to happen, and piano lessons would never be the same again, because now she was special – she was his alone, and they were bound together by their shared love of the piano.

After Monday night's regular *Pick-a-Box*, Prue vanished to her bedroom, and presently Sandra said goodnight too. Don and

Angela remained in their armchairs, with newspapers and books, Ginger curled in his usual position on Don's lap. The house sank into a peaceful silence.

Sandra pulled on a sloppy joe, tied her hair in a ponytail, and ventured quietly, secretly into the darkened street. Clouds blew across a sliver of moon and it was deeply shadowed beneath the occasional trees. Only fifteen minutes if I run to his flat and back, she figured – no one will miss me.

Quickly her sandshoes bore her along the footpath – thankfully it wasn't raining – but the wind blew and she clutched her arms tightly around herself. As she ran, she counted her footsteps, keeping time with every breath. Each gateway opened to gloomy gardens, impenetrable bushes, ghostly trees lit by the street lights; smell of burnt leaves in the roadside gutters. A rustle in the shrubbery made her jump and Sandra's heart leapt with fright before the black shape of a cat streaked across the road. This was no stroll in the friendly Curradeen bush, to cycle home at dusk. This was the city, and in it, she was the stranger.

No light burned in his front room, the flat was in darkness. Mister L'estrange was not at home. Her heart hammered in her chest at the uselessness of her impulsive expedition, the fear that her teacher might suddenly return, see her riveted to the footpath. What an idiot she'd look. She imagined her mother saying, 'Mad! Stark, raving mad.'

As fast as she had sped to stand below the windows of his flat, she ran home, slipping carefully inside, sure that no one had the slightest idea she'd gone out.

Angela met her in the hallway, surprise written all over her face. 'Where on earth have you been?'

'I went for a walk—' Sandra commenced lamely.

'A *walk*! Don't you know what time it is? I don't know what's got into you lately, Sandra. Half the time you walk around with your head in a cloud.'

Ruefully, Sandra heard her mother call her 'Sandra'. But there was nothing she could say, no way to explain. 'I won't do it again, Mum,' she offered. 'I'm trying to think, that's all.'

'You'd better do your thinking at home from now on, and no more of this dashing about after dark.' And Angela shut the front door with a decisive click.

If only Emilia was here… back home in Curradeen, Sandra would've hopped on her bicycle and in no time, she'd be sitting beside Emmy in her comfy bedroom, unloading all her worrisome thoughts. If it was anyone else but Mister L'estrange, she could confide in Aunt Meredith. Now, Carol was the only friend she might tell, but they had never swapped their secrets – just aimless chit-chat, as her mother called it.

She longed for tomorrow. At her lesson tomorrow she would have him all to herself.

23 Tyrell St, Randwick
8 Oct. 61.

Dear Emilia,

I'm sorry that your parents won't let you be a marching girl, you were so excited. I've seen on TV when there are competitions and some of the teams are really big. Maybe your parents will think about it and change their minds.

I hope you will be able to stay over the holidays. I am already planning things for us to do, we can go to Bronte or Bondi beach, not to Coogee or Cronulla as that's where all the lairy girls from school go. Bondi is famous and I can show you the mermaid statues sitting on a big rock at the end of the beach. We'll go to the shops in town and you can meet Aunt Meredith and maybe she'll take us to one of her favourite cafes. It's going to be great fun.

I have got used to school now. Dad says it's about time. He thinks that everyone should settle down. That's what all the teachers say, "Settle down now!" Maybe he should've been a teacher as he's always talking about education. He says I am growing up and high school is serious.

I hope you can visit, write and tell me you can. There's so much to talk about.

Love from Sandra XOX

"Ferrari's Farm,"
Curradeen, N.S.W.
15th Oct.

Dear Sandra,

I am still upset that I can't be a marching girl. I know I would have been good at marching and the uniform we thought of was beautiful because we looked at lots of pictures of marching girls in America and Australia and ours was better.

You are truly my best friend but I want to be with other girls too and do something all of us together so I will feel good. We are the only Italian family here and I still get called wog or dago by some boys especially. They are so rude, I yell back at them but I know it makes it worse. I will have to put up with it but sometimes I get lonely like you.

I'm not allowed to visit in the holidays, Mamma says I have to help at home. Nothing is going right, boo hoo.

Love from Emilia XXXOOO

Seven.

They chose a small table in the crowded Caffé Sport in Norton Street. Outside, several Vespa scooters were propped against the kerb. Sandra liked the babble of voices, the rapid Italian language always reminding her of the Ferrari family. She felt sure that Mrs Ferrari and her mother would love this 'Little Italy'. But now Emilia wasn't allowed to visit in the holidays and they were both so disappointed.

Meredith ordered coffee and *limonata*, and sat gazing into the middle distance. A waiter hovered, and Sandra wondered if it was because Aunt Meredith looked so lovely today: red hair scooped up with slide combs, a scarf knotted at her neck, a swing skirt, her ankle-tied sandals tucked under her chair. The usual jangle of bracelets slid up and down her arms. Auntie had said 'the worst is yet to come,' about her story of William and Sandra was beginning to think she would never hear how the story finished ... or *if* it finished.

'I know what you're going to say, Sandra. You're so transparent, darling,' Meredith laughed, motioning to the waiter that they didn't need him now.

'I want to know about Austinmer, and I want to know what happens to William. Please?'

Meredith addressed her next comment to her short black coffee. 'I can certainly tell you about Austinmer, but I'm not sure about the rest. My story has rather taken off from when I first wanted to show you the comparison with your Nick and my William and our first loves.'

'But you can't stop right in the middle!'

Gleefully she heard Meredith exhale a long breath as she relented. 'Austinmer is a place ... We used to drive there on a weekend. We'd take a picnic, and swim in the ocean pool.'

'But where is it?'

'South of Sydney, north of Wollongong. It's a popular place at the weekend because it's not too far from the city, but far enough away to escape the crowds. A few houses, a little beach. I took that photo of Will the last time we went there. You recognized my old Ford, didn't you?'

Sandra nodded. 'Why did you never go there again?' She sipped her drink, thinking perhaps if she kept her gaze turned away from Aunt Meredith's face, it might help her to keep speaking.

'As you know, William missed out on fighting in the war, so in 1950 when Australia became involved in the Korean War, he saw it as his chance to do something good, to prove he was worth something to people like my parents who thought he was no use – a rich boy who would never amount to anything.'

'He sounds like a good man.'

Meredith smiled. 'Indeed, a very good man.'

It wasn't the answer Sandra had expected with her innocent question about Austinmer. Korea ... a far-away place. 'Anyway, why Korea, and why did there have to be another war?' she asked.

'Hmm, how can I put it ... when Japan was defeated in the Second World War, Korea was divided in half. The Soviet army was in the north and the United States army was in the south. But in 1950 the north invaded the south—'

'Golly, it sounds complicated.'

'It's very complicated, but I'll try to keep it simple. The United Nations asked for international help for South Korea, and Australia agreed.'

'What did William do?' Sandra encouraged, hoping she didn't sound pushy.

'Will volunteered. Because he'd been in the army, he was accepted immediately and shipped out towards the end of 1950. Austinmer was our last little holiday together.'

'That's really sad. But he came back, didn't he?'

'Yes, he came back, with terrible stories about the conflict. He said winter was like fighting against another battalion. They lived with snow storms, frozen rice paddies and rivers, and icy winds from Siberia that cut like a razor. And frostbite ... William was lucky a British soldier gave him some warmer clothes than his own army issue. Then in summer the heat was stifling. Although there was an armistice in 1953, he didn't come home till a year later.'

Meredith beckoned the waiter. 'Would you like something else?' she asked Sandra.

'A coffee, maybe?'

'Then a cappuccino for you.' Meredith ordered their coffees and a sweet *biscotti* each. For a while she didn't speak, then she said, 'You know, Sandra, I have to remind myself that you're only fifteen, you have no experience ... don't you think it's better to wait—'

'No, I don't,' Sandra objected. 'You've started to tell me all about William, how can you stop now?'

'Another time.' She nodded a thank you as the waiter slid their coffees onto the table. 'How do you like your cappuccino?'

'Mmm, Nick and I tried cappuccinos on our day in Sydney last year. I like it, especially the topping.'

'Ah, the *cap*. Some people choose it just for that.' She smiled at Sandra across the table, 'I like what you're wearing this morning – pedal pushers with that neat little blouse and flatties – it really suits you, such pretty colours.'

'Auntie! Don't change the subject. What about William and the war?'

Meredith removed one slide comb, jammed it back firmly in her hair. 'No, I'm not telling you any more. It's getting right away from the story of how William and I met and how we parted. Another day, perhaps.'

'Okay, I'm sorry it makes you sad. But William came home and that was wonderful, wasn't it?'

'Like a miracle.' Meredith drained her coffee cup and fluttered her fingers to farewell the waiter. 'Come on, we're going.'

As she reached for her tote bag, a familiar voice called, 'Hello, Meredith!'

To Sandra's huge surprise, Mister L'estrange magically appeared beside their table.

'Hello Sandra, how are you?' He held the back of a chair as if he might sit down.

'Oh, Eric, I'm sorry, we're just leaving.' Meredith extended her hand to briefly hold his, a faint blush colouring her cheeks. 'It's nice to see you again.'

'You too, Meri, always so beautiful,' he said. 'I'll call you tonight, *ciao ciao*. Bye Sandra.'

'*Ciao,* Eric,' Meredith called over her shoulder as she and Sandra made their way between the crowded tables.

Sandra glanced back to see Mister L'estrange ordering a coffee. With his black hair, slacks and casual jacket, he blended very nicely with the Italian style of the café, and she felt a stab of envy for her aunt.

When they reached her car, Meredith flashed her a smile. 'Your piano teacher! Life's funny, isn't it? I've often seen him when I'm buying groceries, then one night we met at the Trocadero, and I had great fun with his crowd of friends. He's a very good dancer.'

It was as if Sandra had fallen flat on her face, all the wind knocked out of her chest. Meredith never talked about her friends, and now all of a sudden she knew her music teacher. He'd called her *Meri* and said he'd phone her. 'Always so beautiful!' he'd said. Then how many times had they met, how many dances?

Still shocked, she couldn't help the rising tide of jealousy. Her time shared with him over the blue teapot was precious. How could she share him with Meredith? It would change everything. Meredith would whisk him away and Sandra would have nobody. At the same time, she knew it was foolish. Meredith deserved to have fun and be happy. She'd seen the sparkle in her aunt's eyes; she deserved to finally have someone special. But Mister L'estrange?

Meredith glanced briefly at Sandra as she started the car. 'You've gone quiet. Is it because of Mister L'estrange? You like him, don't you?'

She pulled away from the kerb with a jerk of gears. There was nothing Sandra could say in response to Meredith's logical comment.

In another couple of years she'd be old enough to go dancing too. Ha, as if her mother would ever allow it. Not in a million years.

'Saturday 21 Oct. 61.

Dear Emilia,

I've just had the biggest shock. Aunt Meredith knows my music teacher! Today we went to a cafe in Leichhart and Mr. L'estrange suddenly arrived. They met at the Trocadero and they <u>danced</u> together. They were so friendly. I can't help it but I'm sad that he might like her. I don't have any friends except Carol (sort of) and my special days are going to piano lessons and out with Auntie.

I didn't tell you that one night I sneaked out and stood in the street below his flat because I wanted to see him even for a tiny second at the window but all the lights were out and he wasn't home. I was scared to death in the dark. Sorry but I just <u>had</u> to tell you, because I can't talk to Auntie about it. I feel so stupid, but I feel sad too, because it's as if Nick has just slipped out of sight. I cared so much for him but I've given up because I know I'm never going to see him again.

I'm sorry this is long and probably boring, I miss you Emmy, I <u>really really</u> miss you, and I wish you were coming to stay.

Love from stupid Sandra XOX

"Ferrari's Farm,"
27 Oct. 61.

Dear Sandra,

It isn't stupid but it's not right because him and your auntie are much older. You loved Nick, and you wanted to see him again, but you can't, so you can write to me whenever you feel awful and I'll try to help. Do you love your music teacher now?

Pa says I am allowed to go to the pictures with Lofty <u>if Mamma comes with us</u>. I can't believe Pa would make me do that, I would look so silly everyone would laugh at me. I can't tell Lofty the reason that's why I won't go out with him. I am 15 years old and because my parents are Italian they make me feel like a child.

I decided not to confess to the priest that Roger kissed me, because I didn't kiss him back so I didn't do any thing wrong. Nonna says I should confess more often but I don't think I have anything to confess. I don't reckon my thoughts are bad just because I don't agree with Pa.

I am working real hard at school because the Intermediate is soon and Pa still says I have to pass everything or leave school. I did well in the half-yearly so why does he say that?

Your father talks about education and my father talks about the shop. Fathers can be unkind but I suppose they are only trying to help.

Good luck in the exams.

Love from your friend forever
Emilia XXX

3rd. November, 61.

Dear Emilia,

Thank you for being so clever about Auntie and Mr. L. I know you're right and I will try not to ever think about it again. Sometimes I get all mixed up.

You can't go to the pictures with Lofty and your mother, that's <u>awful</u>! But you can go skating with him and to the Silver Moon, so it's not all bad. I think confession sounds frightening, and why tell on yourself when you can go out and do it again? I would hate to have to confess!!!

Aunt Meredith told me more of her story, it's like a love story in a film when her boyfriend went away to fight in the Korean War. I think it's going to have a sad ending even though he came home. I've seen a photograph and he's very handsome. His name is William.

We went to see "North by North West" at the Ritz and Dad came too. I love Cary Grant. Eva Marie Saint has beautiful white-blonde hair. It was very scary when the plane chased him through the corn crop, and also when they're hanging on the cliff, I nearly had to shut my eyes.

My final piano exam is tomorrow, but I'm OK about it.
I've got 2 new pieces and Mozart's sonata. I hated it when
Mr. L first told me to learn it.
Eek, exams! Good luck for yours too!
Lots of Love from
Sandra XXX

"Ferrari's Farm."
9 /11/ 61.

Dear Sandra,

There was a rumour going round school that the roller skate rink will close and now it's true. They say not enough people use it because its old but we know where the cracks and wobbly bits are and it's somewhere for us kids to have fun. The owner of the land wants to build a shed to sell tractors. Boo hoo.

The new swimming pool should be ready by summer, fingers crossed. I'm getting good at swimming. I don't ride my bike much anymore. I wish we got films like you.

I hope your auntie's boyfriend was all right after the war.

love from Emilia XOX

4

In the quiet of evening after dinner, Sandra went to look for her father in the garden. Since Meredith told her a little about William going to the Korean War, disturbing thoughts had plagued her. Why didn't anyone talk about the war – wasn't that the best way to make sure it never happened again?

She found him seated beneath the peach tree. The warmth of the spring day had passed with sunset and he was stretched out on the garden seat, puffing on his pipe. He shifted along to make a space for Sandra.

'This is very pleasant,' he said. 'For once we don't have to drive hundreds of miles for Christmas, and …' he breathed out a stream of smoke, 'I can watch the tennis at home.'

A smell of newly mown lawn filled the garden; an occasional drift of tobacco. Sandra kicked off her sandals and dug her toes into the warm grass. Should she let her father know that Auntie had told her all about William … but how else to begin?

With a glance at her father, she said, 'Dad, can I ask you a question?'

Don smiled. 'You can ask me anything you like, you know that.'

'Auntie told me she had a friend called William who went to fight in the Korean War—' She hesitated and Don pre-empted the question.

'So Meredith's told you about William, has she? Your mother says there's a photo of him in her bedroom.'

'I asked Auntie about the photo and she told me about how they met, because she said it was like me and Nick and how we each had to say goodbye …' She rushed on, before words failed her. 'She wanted me to keep the story of William a secret—'

'That sounds like your Aunt Meredith. She can be melodramatic at times. Still, it was all pretty shocking. Your mother doesn't know the full story – she never approved of how Meredith ran off – but the last couple of years she's swept it under the carpet.' He continued to puff on his pipe.

This was going to take some digging. 'But Dad, if William came home and the Korean War ended not that long ago, why doesn't anyone talk about it? I've never heard anything, even in school.'

'It's a mystery to me. I can only think perhaps it was too soon after World War Two. Around forty thousand of our forces died back then – that's a huge loss for a country of only seven million or so. In the shadow of that global war, maybe people didn't see the Korean War as a *real* war.'

'You've never said anything either. So if it wasn't a *real* war, tell me what happened?'

Don didn't immediately speak as he considered where to start. It was true that no one seemed to talk about the war these days, least of all Meredith.

'Well…' he began. 'Since 1910 the Empire of Japan controlled all of Korea, but after Japan's defeat in 1945, America, with Soviet agreement, divided Korea into roughly equal halves at the 38th Parallel—'

'Auntie told me that.'

'All right, so you know all about it?'

'No, sorry, Dad.'

'Then please don't interrupt when I'm trying to think. In the south, the new Republic of Korea was supported by America, and in the north, the Korean Democratic People's Republic, supported by the Soviet Union. By 1949 both the Soviets and Americans had withdrawn their armies—'

'She said it was complicated.'

'That's true. The story goes there was a civil war when thousands of Koreans died fighting each other. There were supposed to be elections within a year to unify the country, and although the United Nations declared the Republic of Korea in the south as the only *legal* government, in 1950, with Soviet and Chinese back-up, North Korea invaded the South to try to bring the entire country under Communist rule.'

Don paused as he struck a match to relight his pipe. 'South Korean forces and the American forces that rushed to help were pushed down towards the southern tip of Korea. It wasn't

101

looking good, so the United Nations called for international support...'

Sandra resisted a comment that Auntie had also told her this. Instead, she said, 'Is that when William volunteered?'

'Hold your horses, I'm getting to it... Menzies announced we'd send troops, along with Britain and New Zealand, to fight under British command. He was afraid the commies would infiltrate the trade unions and the Labor Party – the so-called *Reds under the Beds*. Menzies was very against the Communist Party of Australia and dead keen on Britain testing bombs in the middle of Australia. It was very divisive.'

'I *have* heard of Reds under the Beds.'

'The United Nations gave command of the troops to Douglas MacArthur, the famous American general, and together with the South Koreans, they pushed the North Korean army through the mountains and right up to the border with China. That certainly put the cat among the pigeons and the Chinese invaded – an enormous army that pushed the U.N. and South Korean troops all the way down south again.'

'Did William talk to you about it?'

'When he eventually came home... the only time we spoke together. After that day I didn't see him again. We sat over a beer or two, and while he was talking, his hands shook so badly that his glass rattled on the table. He said at night they could hear the Chinese communicating with whistles and bugles, and it was terrifying because they knew what was coming...'

For a moment, Don didn't speak, then he said, 'Think of it, Sandy, thousands of Chinese – wave after wave charging with mortar and rifle fire, some of them carrying only buckets of grenades. The way William described it – my god, the hand-to-hand fighting—'

'Did William fight like that, too?' She held her breath, afraid of the answer, regretful that she'd wanted her father to explain the war.

'I have no doubt, William too.'

While Don drew on his pipe, Sandra picked idly at a paint bubble on the garden seat. Over the back fence, she heard the murmur of their neighbours' voices, the chatter of birds as they settled for the night in nearby camphor laurel trees.

'If General MacArthur was so famous, how come the fighting was so terrible?' she asked.

'MacArthur wanted to take the war from North Korea into China. He wanted to use the bomb, but President Truman worried it would lead to world war three – Russia had tested an atom bomb in 1949, China had gone Communist – so in 1951 Truman sacked him.'

Sandra rummaged in her brain for something to say. Her father had painted a frightening picture of a remote war that had dragged people like William away, then sent him home, only to inexplicably vanish from Meredith's life. She felt compelled to ask, 'What happened after MacArthur got the sack?'

'Fighting went to and fro till the armistice was signed in 1953, and Korea remained cut in half at the demilitarized zone. We lost over three hundred Australians, but thousands of Americans died – there's still no final count, even today. As for the Chinese and Koreans, who knows… a million or more? And the poor civilians trying to escape the bombing and strafing, nowhere to go, everything destroyed.'

Her father's story was getting worse and worse. Sandra wiggled her toes in the grass, finding comfort in the simple barefoot pleasure. 'Can you tell me more about William?'

Don frowned into the bowl of his pipe. 'He was pretty cut up. I don't know how those blokes managed after the war – after any war. He told me that one day American planes accidentally dropped napalm – that's jellied petrol – on some Australian troops. He saw their terrible burns. Two men died that he knew of. A mistake, for god's sake!'

Silence settled over the garden seat, Sandra's head a muddle of ugly thoughts. 'Auntie didn't tell me anything horrible like that. All she said was William came home after the armistice. So how come we don't see him, ever?'

After a long pause, Don said, 'You asked me about the war … as for William, I think that should remain Meredith's story. If she wants you to know, she'll tell you.'

He puffed on his pipe and it gurgled unhappily. 'The borders on either side of the two and a half mile-wide demilitarized zone are probably the heaviest fortified borders in the world.'

Dissatisfied, Sandra continued picking at the paint bubble, turmoil in her mind. She heaved a breath, asked: 'How do wars happen, Dad? How do people get like that?'

Don took her hand, held it loosely in the warm evening. 'Power, greed … possession. Religious beliefs. Trade. Lots of theories, dear, lots of theories. And people become swept up in the conflicts and lose sight of themselves. Strange things happen – a couple of months ago, East Germany built a wall *overnight*, right around West Berlin – it's hard to understand sometimes. So we've still got the Cold War but perhaps that'll be a balance between the great powers, and perhaps this time, Neville Chamberlain's "peace for our time" might last.'

Sandra could hardly see her father, close by in the fading light; the rare comfort of his hand holding hers. The Cold War didn't mean anything to her right now, or Chamberlain, whoever he was. Not tonight. She tried to blot out the picture of men rushing at each other, filled with furious efforts to kill, terrified of dying. William among them … his face from the photograph.

Tomorrow was her music exam. Concentrate on that now.

'I hope that helps answer your question?' Don tapped his pipe on the garden seat. 'We'd better go in before the mozzies find us, eh?'

eight.

Mister L'estrange opened the letter with Sandra's practical exam results, and read it to her while she sat staring at the keyboard, not daring to look at him. She had tried hard, and although she'd wanted to play the Mozart sonata better, she was positive that Schubert's *Moment Musicaux* had been good, Handel was good and she had survived the scales and sight-reading. At the conclusion when she said thank you, she thought she detected a smile twitch the corner of the examiner's mouth and mentally crossed her fingers.

'You've done well,' Mister L'estrange finally commented. 'You've surprised me, Sandra.' She ignored the way he said *Sarrndra*, and waited for him to continue. 'You've surprised me with your compositions,' he repeated, 'and in return, I have a surprise for you.'

23 Tyrell St., Randwick.
14 /11/ 61.

Dear Emilia,

You'll never guess what! Mr. L has tickets for a concert at the Town Hall and he invited me to go because he said I've worked hard and my exam results were <u>excellent</u>! Mum says I can go, because it's very special to be invited to such an important concert even though he is much older than me and Dad says age has nothing to do with it, it's all part of my <u>education</u>.

I'll see Igor Stravinsky conduct the music he wrote for the ballet "The Firebird". I've never heard of it but Stravinsky is a world famous Russian composer and Mr. L says his music is inspirational. I think he must be a very old man. Mum says I'm allowed to buy kitten heels and have my hair set!

And also guess what, Dad drew Lord Fury in the bank sweep for the Melbourne Cup and won £10.00. A horse with a name like that deserved to win. He beat the other horses by far and gets over £20,000 !!

I asked Dad about the Korean War and he told me about the fighting. William came home, so he was lucky. But I still don't know the end of the story.

The exams were OK. When I finish early I worry that I left something out. We get our results before we break up. How did you go?

It's too bad the skating rink will close and they just shut it without asking.

Love from Sandra XOXOX

"Ferrari's Farm."
18/11/ 61.

Dear Sandra,

I like the stamp you stuck on with the 100th Melbourne Cup horse Archer. Maybe you miss horses. It's been really busy at home with the shop and that. I have to cook dinner sometimes when Nonna is tired and clean house for Mamma because she gets tired too.

I studied my subjects very hard but I was so nervous before the exams I don't know what my results will be like. I'm sure I did some maths back to front but Pa says that's not possible. I know I did alright in English because I liked the questions. I think that's a good sign but I'm afraid I will have to leave school.

When I asked Pa about the Korean War he said "Non più guerra, no no no" and he wouldn't talk about it. Mamma shooshed me because in the big world war they had to hide so they didn't get shot. I better not ask any more.

You lucky thing to go to a concert, tell me all about it.

Love from Emilia
XOXO

Sandra's wardrobe doors hung open as she pulled out several summer dresses, muttering to herself as she searched for a suitable one to wear. But she was surprised to discover that none would fit – they were all too tight in the bodice, too short in the skirt.

Dressed in her underwear, she appraised herself in the mirror: same long, fair hair and urky brown eyes, but not the same skinny self – the bony bits no longer stuck out, her hips subtly curved, and no one could call her bust "bee stings" any more, like at the old Curradeen pool change rooms.

Secretly pleased, she moaned to her mother, 'All my clothes are too tight ... Ooh, the concert's next week and I've got nothing to wear!'

Angela laughed at the woebegone face. 'What have I been telling you about growing up? We'll ask Aunt Meredith, she's very quick and clever with her sewing machine.'

Down on her knees, Meredith busily pinned up the hem of Sandra's new dress: dark blue cotton with a narrow skirt, cap sleeves, and a cotton sateen jacket that would have a matching blue-black border, Chanel-style.

With a glance up at Sandra, she remarked, 'I do believe you've grown an inch or more, you're looking very pretty these days.' Sandra gave her a shy smile as Meredith added, 'Sixteen next year, how time flies.'

Meredith's sewing was expert, the dress and jacket fitted perfectly. Sandra saw herself in the mirror with an unfamiliar feeling of satisfaction. She thought she actually looked quite nice, perhaps even pretty, as auntie had said, and it was not too difficult to walk in her new kitten heels after a week's practice around the house. Sandra touched her hair, stiff with spray, the top backcombed higher, then falling in a smooth curl to her shoulders. Brandishing scissors, the hairdresser had insisted short hair was all the fashion, preferably teased into a big bouffant style, but Sandra refused to have it cut, telling her, 'I like it just the way it is, thank you.'

From the foot of the stone stairs leading up to the entrance, under a full moon, the Town Hall loomed above them: all pillars, balconies and windows, topped with its tall clock tower. As she trod the stairs with Mister L'estrange, Sandra thrilled at joining the people crowding into the foyer for such an important event. Their seats were close to the front and fascinated, she gazed at the artistry on every wall and cornice, the decorative ceiling hung with sparkling chandeliers. Behind the orchestra, a massive organ covered the entire end wall, reaching up towards the ceiling. Mister L'estrange had told her once, 'the more you look, the more you see,' and it was certainly true.

A hush enveloped the crowd as the lights dimmed, and applause welcomed Stravinsky's assistant conductor for the first half of the concert.

It passed like a dream – to sit so close, to see the exuberance of the conductor, the row of brass horns, violinists sawing their bows – but lost in the mystery of *Pulcinella* her thoughts drifted. Mustn't fidget, she told herself… sit still, ankles crossed like the queen, try to concentrate. The *Symphony in Three Movements* that followed was dramatic and discordant from the instant the orchestra crashed into the strident allegro opening. She couldn't follow a thread, but the erratic, threatening music grabbed her attention from those first notes, through the calm andante second movement, to the gripping chorus that led to the symphony's abrupt finish. Surrounded by loud applause from the audience, Sandra leaned back in her seat, unsure if she had enjoyed it. Mister L'estrange had told her Stravinsky completed the symphony in 1945, so perhaps it was filled with the noise of war and marching soldiers... all that brass. She should have guessed this would be no Mozart or Schumann.

'You didn't tell me it'd be like that,' she protested as they made their way outside for the interval. 'My ears are still ringing.'

'Stravinsky's Russian, what would you expect? He experienced the turmoil of that era, enormous changes. Good, hmm?' He flicked open a silver case, withdrawing a thin black cigarette, gold-tipped.

They stood with the talkative crowd on the Town Hall steps while he smoked. She liked how her music teacher was dressed – so different to the conservative-looking men in their grey, their pin-striped suits. His suit was a soft, dark cloth, his deep blue tie pinned with a tiny diamond against the white shirt. It was the first time she'd seen his hair slicked back from his forehead – she thought he looked handsome, a little like a gypsy – and he wore the earring. She noticed occasional glances towards him, and again she thrilled to be by his side.

Dropping his cigarette butt into a sand box, he said, 'The first piece after interval is the *Apollon Musagetes*. Stravinsky wrote the score for a ballet. It lasts about half an hour, so be patient and think of the god Apollo and the Muses, hmm?'

Oh, yet another piece before *The Firebird*...

'I should explain the story for *The Firebird – L'Oiseau de Feu*,' Mister L'estrange continued. 'Stravinsky composed it in 1910 for

Serge Diaghilev's Russian Ballet. Tonight, we'll hear only *Berceuse*, the lullaby, and the *Finale*.

'So … it goes like this. A prince captures the Firebird – I believe it was stealing apples – and in exchange for freedom, the Firebird gives him a magical feather to use if he ever needs help, which of course is what happens. Inevitably, he falls in love with a princess, but an evil ogre rules her and all the other creatures—'

'What sort of an ogre?'

'An immortal being … when the prince tells the ogre he wants to marry the princess, they fight and the prince uses his magic feather to escape the wicked ogre and all the evil creatures pursuing him.'

'That's like any old-fashioned fairy story with the baddies chasing the goodies.'

'Exactly. But a Russian fairy story … the Firebird tells him how to kill the ogre by destroying its soul which is kept separately in a magic egg—'

Sandra smothered a giggle. 'How can a soul be inside an *egg*?'

'Never mind that. The Firebird makes the ogre and all his awful creatures dance so strenuously they fall asleep. That's when we'll hear *Berceuse*. The prince destroys the egg so the ogre dies, and in the *Finale* everyone lives happily ever after.' He crushed out his cigarette. 'That's my version of the ballet, not exactly right but enough for now.'

'It's better than reading the program,' Sandra laughed. Mister L'estrange was full of surprises tonight.

'Your favourite composer Claude Debussy was at the very first performance,' he said. 'They became friends and I believe Debussy was some influence on his style of composition. But Debussy also pushed him to honour his Russian roots.'

'To be true to himself?' she suggested.

When the bell rang for the next performance, they returned to their seats. Now she would see the famous Igor Stravinsky himself, who, according to Mister L'estrange, had changed music forever when he composed *The Firebird*.

To excited applause, Stravinsky appeared, pushing through the curtains towards the orchestra: a very short man, bald head, big ears and heavy spectacles, Sandra thought he seemed no taller than her. She watched him make his way to the conductor's podium. Taking careful steps, now he was almost there. Such a bent old man to be conducting a huge orchestra, she wondered would the music be any good?

Mister L'estrange leaned towards her to whisper, 'He's seventy-nine.' For an instant, she smelled his unfathomable scent, felt the puff of breath in her ear, the touch of his shoulder against hers.

As Stravinsky bowed in response to the continued, rapturous applause, she saw how beautifully he was dressed. From his perfect white shirt, waistcoat and white bow tie with a black tailcoat, down to his mirror-shiny shoes, he grew in stature before her eyes, and she recognized her good fortune to be there.

But the *Apollon* ... maybe if she could see the ballet she might like it better. Mister L'estrange wished her to witness Igor Stravinsky conducting *The Firebird*, so it was *Firebird* that she waited for. Violin solo dum-de-dum ... how much longer? She sneaked a look at her piano teacher, noticed his foot almost imperceptibly moving to the rhythm. Finally, a crescendo of strings, it must be near the end ... it would have helped to know the story. The theme repeated itself over and over, fading ... fading ... and *Apollon* ended.

Amid the enthusiastic applause she heard Mister L'estrange say, 'Now for *The Firebird!*'

Stravinsky raised his hands to begin. Into the complete silence of the Town Hall came the singular notes of a solo instrument, sombre and brooding. Sandra held her breath – she had never heard anything like this before – then with a ripple of harp strings, her spirit lifted up and up with the thrilling sweep of violins and cellos, Stravinsky beckoning their entry, his fingers weaving fine lines as if connected to the strings. Again the languorous notes came from the soloist, and then an echo of those hypnotic notes, higher, plaintive, like an answer. Deeply absorbed by the music, Sandra knew it was possible to be transported by those six repeated notes, and beneath it all, a melodious beat like a plucked string that beat in her veins. From the corner of her eye, she saw Mister L'estrange glance at her but when she returned his glance he was again watching the performance.

Stravinsky held up one finger, cocked his head as he listened: mysterious and tremulous strings softly began to descend lower, lower … she hardly breathed, perched on the edge of her seat as the trembling pianissimo descent continued, ever lower until an exciting whirlwind of sound erupted from the entire orchestra. With unexpected sweetness, a surge of strings singing like points of light, flutes that scurried; rushing, urgent, electrifying. Surely this signified optimism? The ogre was dead together with his evil creatures, as Mister L'estrange had described.

Another flick of the fingers as Stravinsky turned a page … finally he stood with his fists moving in unison as he drove the orchestra to the climax of the *Finale*: drums triumphantly beating, building and building to a crescendo, carrying away the audience, carrying Sandra away too as she sat with hands clenched on her knees. Trombones, trumpets, all came together until, with a clash of cymbals and the long-drawn final notes from brass and strings, it was over.

The audience burst into tremendous applause, cheering and shouting as the lights went up. Stravinsky bowed, once, twice, and to the orchestra – smiling, shaking the hand of the first violinist – perhaps relieved that it was done. And it had been magnificent, stunning and unforgettable. Sandra felt her face would split with smiling as Stravinsky vanished behind the curtain, the audience still wildly applauding.

'Like ski poles!' Mister L'estrange laughed with delight as they joined the crowd slowly making its way towards the door. 'He conducted the last few minutes like he was skiing. *Schuss schuss.*' Out in the fresh night air, he turned triumphantly to Sandra, his eyes shining. 'A one in a million chance tonight – you will never hear *The Firebird* like that, ever again. When I hear it, I want to shout and leap with joy!'

In the crowd of people streaming out of the Town Hall, they crossed the road to the Queen Victoria Building, and he asked, 'What did you think? Did you like it? You must tell me.'

'I've never heard anything like it before. What's that strange instrument that played the solo? Oh, I loved that.'

'The bassoon,' Mister L'estrange replied. 'A remarkable instrument, I imagine very difficult to play well, to achieve that supremely beautiful *legato.*'

'And I loved the harp, and there was a piano, and …'she giggled at the memory, 'I heard a tinkly triangle at the end, even with those huge drums.' Sandra turned to look at her teacher, adding shyly, 'thank you for taking me.'

On the edge of the kerb as she tottered beside him, her foot wobbled and almost slipped off the kitten heel. Mister L'estrange quickly grabbed her arm, held her until she regained her balance.

'Pretty shoes can be dangerous,' he said, letting her go. 'Dressed up tonight for Igorrrr, very nice, very dangerous.'

As they walked to the car, for an instant, Sandra considered pretending to stumble off her heel so that he would again rescue her from falling, but Mister L'estrange was on the other side of the footpath, propelling his arms like Stravinsky, laughing, '*schuss schuss*.' Then he said, 'We'll have coffee somewhere and talk about it ... it's impossible to go straight home after such music. *The Firebird* stuns the soul, don't you agree?' Without waiting for her answer, he declared, 'No, no, we'll drive down to the harbour ...'

Bright reflections from buildings near the Quay glittered on the black water. They stood at the rail, where below in the gloom, water slap-slapped against the pilings. People gathered at the wharves for the last ferries that soon would depart. On the opposite shore, Luna Park sparkled near the immense dark curve of the Harbour Bridge.

Sandra could still hear the brooding notes from the bassoon echoing the theme. 'What's it feel like, do you think, to hear music from inside your head, played by an orchestra?' she asked.

'Incredible! Imagine the audience confronted by those sounds at the first performance. I'm sure it would've shattered them, exalted them. The old battle between good and evil: the firebird and the ogre, like opposing religions, or countries at war.' He paused while he lit a cigarette, adding, 'But goodness eventually wins, as it should.'

For a while they stood in silence, the music swarming in Sandra's head. A ferry drew away from the wharf, foam churning as ropes cast off, and eventually the ferry vanished into the open harbour, beyond the glittering reflections.

'Stravinsky was twenty-seven when he composed *The Firebird*, the same age as me,' Mister L'estrange said. 'But I will never write a *Firebird*.'

So, Mister L'estrange was twenty-seven. Sandra tucked that information away in her head. Not so very old. 'But you *have* composed music,' she said. 'The piece you played—'

'Yes, yes, my lyrical compositions – some sonatas, concertos. I've composed for ensembles, but never for an orchestra. I like the intimacy of small groups.'

Sandra gazed around at the brilliance, the colourful neon lights, Mister L'estrange almost a silhouette beside her.

'One day,' he pointed into the darkness, 'On that point of land, the Opera House will be built. Now there's only the beginning, the first stage. One day, you'll go to a concert there, and you might remember tonight when you saw the great Igor Stravinsky conduct his fabulous *Firebird*. Maybe one day you might compose music to be played there, astonishing music, hmm?'

'I'll never forget it,' Sandra sighed. 'Like you said, it stuns the soul. Thank you very much for taking me, Mister L'estrange, I really *really* enjoyed it.'

'I'm glad,' he replied. 'I wanted to show you what can be possible in our lives. You have your music and composition, and that's a gift to treasure and nurture.' He flicked his cigarette butt into the harbour. 'And now I'm going to see you safely home.'

24 / 11 / 61

Dear Emilia
I can't tell you how wonderful the concert was and Stravinsky is such a little old man but he was like a magician and it was so <u>wonderful</u>, I don't think I'll ever hear anything or <u>feel anything</u> like it again. After the concert Mr. L said I might compose astonishing music one day. Maybe that's why I always like making up my own songs? And now I know for sure Mr. L is 27. I think he might like me a little bit.

Auntie made me a new blue dress with a cotton sateen Chanel jacket and I got kitten heels and a new hairdo for the night. Mum bought me a fancy suspender belt to hold up my stockings! All my clothes are too small because I've grown over an inch and Prue isn't taller than me any more.

I'm so glad your parents got the ship to come to Australia because otherwise we might never have met and be best friends.

love from Sandra XOXO

Days later, sprawled in bed, sheet thrown off because it was such a hot night, Sandra went over and over the night of the concert. She'd wanted to stay leaning on the harbour rail with Mister L'estrange, listening to *The Firebird* music in her head. She heard him again, his voice saying remarkable things beside her; pondered his words as she drifted into sleep.

Next lesson, she told herself, I'll ask him to explain more about my new direction, and then he'll make tea in the blue pot and we'll speak about all sorts of things.

7

Since the concert, piano lessons had taken on a more colourful tone as if the air buzzed with inspiration, and Sandra approached her pieces with renewed vigour. She felt she'd grown into them, it was no longer all fiddle-dee-dee, as Mister L'estrange had sharply described it. Lessons were followed by cups of tea – the same golden brew in the blue pot – but no longer accompanied by tears. Mister L'estrange would smoke his cigarette, and always he played a piece for her as a conclusion to the lesson.

'It's my thank you,' he admitted, 'because you've become an excellent pupil and a more interesting girl than one usually meets. I hope you will learn from your Stravinsky experience, hmm?'

Only one more lesson before Mister L'estrange departed for London to visit his family. What's more, he was going to fly!

'I haven't seen my family for nearly three years,' he said. 'Flying will be a new experience. Just think, only eight stops along the way on a big Qantas Boeing 707.'

No lessons until the end of January. Six weeks without Mister L'estrange. Sandra wondered how it would feel to be without him. Strange indeed! One more lesson, then a certain freedom in which she would have all the time in the world for her own compositions – she'd already bought a stack of blank sheets at Palings and a fine black pen.

She closed the front door of the foyer and walked towards the footpath. Light rain was falling, the air thick with humidity – the temperature had reached ninety degrees for several days. She would have to run home as she didn't have an umbrella.

A quick movement under the bushes close by the building caught her eye. Something had darted into the thicket and hidden in the dense foliage. Stooping to see what it was, Sandra was surprised to spy a small grey face with two pointy ears. Blue eyes stared back at her: a kitten, very wet from the rain. As she reached towards it, the kitten tried to escape, but became caught up in leaves and twigs. She clasped the small body, her briefcase slipping to the path as the kitten wriggled and hissed with alarm.

'Poor little thing,' she whispered, stroking the small bony head, feeling the rapid beat of its heart against her breast as the kitten gradually quietened. 'Where's your mother and your brothers and sisters?'

The rain became heavier and Sandra had no choice but to knock on the door of Mister L'estrange's door, kitten and briefcase both clutched firmly to her chest.

'Back again?' he said with surprise, then, 'Good god, what on earth have you got?'

Sandra knelt down to put the kitten on the floor. 'It was hiding under the bushes. What will we do with it?'

'You can take it home instantly… come on, I'll drive you—'

'But we've got a cat, a big ginger cat that would hate a kitten.'

'Hmm. He might even hurt it.' He brushed the hair from his eyes, kneeling as he picked up the kitten to inspect the little creature. His head was close to hers and she smelled the cigarettes, and the other, different, delectable scent. 'It's a female,' he announced, 'and a fleabag.' He set the kitten on its feet, soothing it with gentle strokes of his long fingers. 'She'll need looking after, how can I do that with my students?'

'But can't you keep her until we find the owner?'

Mister L'estrange produced a towel, and Sandra enfolded the kitten in it, wiping the wet fur. It gazed about with its blue eyes while it submitted to being dried.

'You've forgotten that I'm leaving next week, yours is the final lesson. Are you going to look after the kitten then, if no one claims her?'

Sandra suspected it was a rhetorical question but she seized on it. 'Yes! After you've gone I can come every day. It's not far to walk, and school breaks up soon.'

'*Mon Dieu*,' Mister L'estrange sighed. 'I suppose we have no choice, we can't throw kitty into the street again. Perhaps she can stay for a few days, and we'll tape notices here and there. I'll have to give you a key.'

'I'll feed her every day, twice a day...' Sandra paused for breath, with a sudden thought, 'what if no one claims her, what'll we do then?'

'I certainly don't want a cat,' Mister L'estrange replied. 'We'll have to wait and see. Your giant ginger cat may have to learn a lesson in community spirit, but I'll look after her until I leave.'

'I can buy a dirt tray and make her a bed.'

'A cardboard-box lid will do for a tray until tomorrow.' He headed for the kitchen, muttering, 'Newspapers, cat tray, flea powder...' to return with a saucer of warm milk.

When Sandra gently pushed the kitten's chin into it, she experimentally lapped with help from a finger. 'Look at the dear little thing, she's a fast learner. 'I'll call her *Kitty*.'

'Write a song about her. Now take my umbrella and go home.'

Sandra hurried down the stairs again, leaving Mister L'estrange to accommodate the kitten and her fleas as best he could.

Tomorrow she would get her Intermediate exam results. In three weeks it would be Christmas. A whole year had slipped past. Quickly she ran through the sprinkling rain, her spirits surging with happiness.

Still breathless with excitement, Sandra dumped her briefcase in the hallway. Her parents were enjoying their regular sherry before the six o'clock news. Don was home early for a change – he would soon be on annual holidays and a relieving manager would take over. Busy with homework, Prue sat at the dining table.

Startled at Sandra's noisy entry, everyone looked up.

Angela frowned, noticing the time. 'You're very late today, Sandy—'

'Guess what! I found a kitten after my lesson, and Mister L'estrange says he'll look after her until he goes away.'

'Goes away?' Angela was taken aback. 'What about your lessons? Where's he going?'

'Sorry, I forgot to tell you. Anyway, we don't have lessons in the holidays. He's going to London next week to see his family for Christmas. He's *flying!*'

'Flying? That'll cost him a pretty penny.'

'A break will be good for you,' Don said. 'You can do some of that composing we've heard about. It sounds jolly good from what your teacher told us.'

'Oh Don, I'm very disappointed Sandy doesn't want to pursue performance,' Angela said, 'when that's all she's talked about for years. I simply don't understand.'

'We can't deny Sandra has always played her own pieces alongside her studies—'

'Tinkled,' Angela interrupted. 'She's *tinkled.*'

'He's a skinny fellow,' Don went on as if he hadn't heard Angela's objections. 'And that hair!' He chuckled, 'Rather sissy, if you ask me. What do you think of his earring, eh?'

'I don't mind it,' Sandra said defensively, feeling a blush creep up her cheeks, inwardly fuming at this criticism.

Side-stepping an awkward situation, Don said, 'If he's such a good teacher and your headmistress says he's brilliant, I don't see that it matters much what a man looks like.'

'Tell us about the kitten?' Prue pleaded.

'She's got beautiful grey fur with blue eyes—'

'Cats don't have blue eyes.'

'Kittens do. Mister L'estrange thinks she's about two months old. We're putting "found" notices up with our phone number because he'll be away. And I'll have a key so I can feed her when he's gone.'

Pleased that an argument had been avoided, Don said, 'Well, it's all right with me. With luck, someone will turn up for her.'

'Maybe I'd better speak to him about it,' Angela said. 'What do you think, Don?'

'Sandra's worked it out. If her teacher's happy to let her have a key to feed the cat, I don't see a problem.'

Prue closed her schoolbooks. 'I'd like a kitten.' She came to perch on her father's armchair. 'Please, Dad? Ginger won't play anymore; he won't even chase a bow on a string.'

'No more cats,' Angela said. 'Poor Ginger wouldn't like it, and that's that.'

'Then can I have a rabbit?'

'Now you're being silly,' Angela said with finality.

23 Tyrell St., Randwick.
5th. December, 61.

Dear Emilia,

Today I found the dearest little kitten hiding in a bush outside Mr. L's flat. It's a girl and I called her Kitty and he'll keep her until we find who she belongs to. He goes to England soon for the holidays and if nobody claims Kitty he'll give me a key to go and feed her. He put notices in the shops but I hope no one phones.

He says he doesn't want a cat but I know he likes her. Mum says we can't have another cat because of Ginger.

All the girls in my class wished me Happy Christmas — maybe school will be nicer next year. Carol gave me Cashmere Bouquet soap so I got her lavender talcum powder. I posted you a card and a tiny present.

Did you get your results yet? It's nearly the holidays and I wish you were coming.

Love from Sandra XOX

Don tossed some how-to-vote cards onto the breakfast table. 'We have to vote this Saturday. Bob Menzies is darned unpopular these days. Unemployment is up and it'll be a miracle if the Liberal party's re-elected.

'We don't want the other fellow, the Labor man,' Angela said, 'that Arthur Calwell.'

'That's true, but the Coalition's in a black hole. Holt's budget caused plenty of pain – I don't know what they're going to do about it.' Don cut off the top of his boiled egg. 'Pass the salt and pepper, please.'

Prue pushed the cruets across the table. 'What about the kitten? If nobody owns her, can we keep her?'

'We can't,' Sandra said. 'Like Mum said last night, Ginger's too old and he wouldn't like it. And we don't want a rabbit either.'

'So?'

'How would I know?' Sandra said. 'Wait and see.'

If they didn't hurry up eating their cornflakes and toast, they'd miss the bus.

"Ferrari's Farm."
11th December, 61.

Dear Sandra,

I passed all my exams and I got good marks so I will go into Fourth Year. You should have seen Nonna dance in the kitchen in her long skirt. Pa was happy too and now he tells all his customers that I passed the Intermediate.

I got your card and I love the stockings, they are the best I ever had. I posted you a card with a little china angel and the Glory to God special Christmas stamp.

Guess what!! I am so happy happy hapy I am allowed to visit you after New Year !!! I think Nonna talked Pa into it. I am excited to come on the train. Can we go to the mermaid beach, that sounds lovely and will I get to meet your auntie? If you still have Kitty when I come, maybe I can cuddle her? I never had a pet, she sounds really cute.

Everything is going good now. The pictures with Lofty was alright, we saw an Elvis film and it was fun, whenever there's kissing the kids yell and scream and throw Jaffas until the usher shines a torch. For muck up day someone put a man's undies up the flagpole and there was a big fuss until the kids owned up.

Love from Emilia XOX

The sound of a piano filtered through Mister L'estrange's front door as Sandra reached the top step. She had been on her way home from school, but the temptation to inspect Kitty was too great, especially knowing that Wednesday was her teacher's final day for lessons. Bad luck if he was out, but she'd crossed her fingers he would be home.

As she knocked on the door, to her surprise she heard Mister L'estrange call, 'It's not locked, come in.' He brought the piece to a close, half-turned from the piano. 'I thought you might be tempted to visit Kitty today.' he said.

'But where is she?'

'Can't you see?'

He indicated his knees, and Sandra saw the kitten curled under a fold of his loose shirt. He'd said most emphatically, 'I certainly don't want a cat,' and now Kitty snoozed quite at home on his lap.

Mister L'estrange was greatly amused. 'She likes Schubert, I sent her to sleep with *Cradle Song*. And she likes your John Field *Nocturne*. Watch, I'll play it again.'

As he played the first notes, Kitty roused from her doze and put a paw on the keyboard.

'See, she likes treble notes best.' He laughed as Kitty batted his fingers. 'B flat major, a cheerful and optimistic key.' He uncurled the kitten from his knees and slipped her onto the floor. 'I stuck some notices close by my flat and around the shops. Her owner might see one and telephone, hmm?'

'And if no one does?'

'She's yours!'

4

Mister L'estrange had scarcely departed for England – the door had scarcely closed behind him – when Sandra next visited Kitty. She felt most peculiar walking up the stairs, knowing she would insert the long brass key in the lock for the very first time, turn it until she heard the click of the latch, and she would be standing alone in his flat.

She turned the key, carefully pushed the door open a crack. Where was Kitty? She peeked inside, then slid into the room, being very careful in case the kitten was close by and tried to escape, but there was no sign of her. The lounge room was tidy as usual, but Kitty was nowhere to be seen. She called, 'puss puss puss?' with no response. She would have to search, room by room.

In the kitchen, the bowls on the floor were empty, so Kitty must be somewhere – she couldn't get lost in a flat. On one wall was a colourful poster of a bullfighter swinging his cape at a black bull, its horns pointing dramatically towards his chest. She supposed Mister L'estrange must have seen a bullfight, perhaps this very one, but the idea of the bull's death was ugly and she turned away. She had called him a gypsy…

The piano was in the next room and curled on the stool was the sleeping kitten, tucked into a small ball on a cushion. Sandra bent close and saw that Kitty had her eyes open a slit, watching her. 'You're only pretending to sleep,' she laughed, cuddling the kitten. 'Perhaps you miss Mister L'estrange,' she told the kitten. 'Well, I'm going to miss him too.'

The thought had crept up on her. She *would* miss her teacher. Almost every week for the entire year she sat beside him for lessons, which had developed into chats over the blue teapot until it was time to go home. She thought of her mad helter-skelter dash to his flat that night, hoping for … what? Each night she lay on her pillows, wondering if perhaps her teacher might like her in a romantic way, regardless of Aunt Meredith. She remembered how auntie raised her eyebrows when she described the cups of tea after each lesson.

Putting Kitty on her lap, she sat at the piano. Mister L'estrange had played *Cradle Song* for the kitten, so Sandra played several bars from memory and Kitty obediently settled. After that, she played some harmonies and chords with no particular direction before deciding to further explore the flat. Why not, she thought, and even if I move something one half inch he will never know because he's away for so long.

The bathroom … here was her chance to investigate the intriguing little perfume bottle. Mister L'estrange had taken some things, but the squat little bottle was still there, next to a shaving brush. Her fingers reached for it, inspected the writing imbedded on the glass: Toujours fidèle, and beneath the name she read d'orsay.

In her heart she knew it had to be the fragrance that she often detected, regardless of his cigarette. She withdrew the odd little stopper – he would never know that she'd opened it – sniffed it, upended the bottle to dab onto a finger: an orangey scent, woody and vaguely sweet. With her finger, Sandra put a little perfume on her neck and wrists, as her mother did with her *Evening in Paris*. It smelt delicious, as if she could breathe it forever, eat it, dissolve in it. Intoxicated with the experience, she closed her eyes. Perhaps another little dab ... then slowly, very carefully, she replaced the bottle.

Next, she picked up the shaving brush, still slightly damp – perhaps he shaved in the morning like her father. In front of the mirror, she drew the brush across her cheek, felt its cool, luxurious softness. A few hours ago, Mister L'estrange had stroked his cheeks, his throat with this brush ...

It only remained for Sandra to look in her teacher's bedroom. She had promised herself, I will *not* go in, I will see all I want to see from the doorway, but she couldn't help wandering in, seeing at a glance the simple way he lived: a double bed covered in a plain blue blanket, a couple of pillows; bedside cabinet with a lamp, the small wardrobe; a desk, several books and journals with foreign titles she didn't recognize. She didn't dare open the wardrobe, although she longed to see what clothes hung on its hooks.

The bed... It drew her irresistibly and she sat on the edge. If she rested her head on the pillow just for a minute ... gently she tilted to one side, let herself sink down so the pillows were beneath her cheek, all the time thinking: I shouldn't be here ... in a moment I will get up. She spread her arms and legs like a star, delighted to discover: this is what it feels like to lie on Mister L'estrange's bed, rest on his pillows. *Eric:* she ran her tongue around the name, lengthened the first syllable, tested it on the air, but still with the thought: I should get up, this is wrong. But it felt so comfortable to lie stretched on his bed – she wondered did he sleep on his back or would he lie curled like a child? Turning her face into the pillow, she breathed in hard, trying in vain to find the scent of the man who had slept there only last night, feel his skin smooth beneath her fingers, the silken hair that she'd never touched.

Kitty suddenly jumped onto the bed, regarding her with curiosity. Shocked, Sandra swung shaky legs off the bed, smoothed pillows and blanket to perfection so not a trace, not a single fair hair remained to tell tales. After a quick glance to ensure the bedroom was exactly as she'd found it, she left, calling, 'puss puss puss?'

Angela waved a piece of paper. 'A woman phoned about the kitten. Will you ring back to arrange for her to visit?' She gave Sandra the note, saw tears welling in her daughter's eyes.

'I'm sorry, I know you wanted to keep Kitty.' She put her arm around Sandra's shoulders, kissed the top of her head. 'But you told me your teacher didn't want a cat, and it's not fair to Ginger. We really can't.'

So soon. She had only fed the kitten for one day and now maybe Kitty would be taken away.

13th Dec. 61.

Dear Emilia,

I have to write to you because you're the only one I can tell. After Mr. L'estrange left this morning, when I went to feed Kitty I couldn't help lying on his bed and I felt so melting I thought I'd faint. Have you ever felt like that? I should never have gone in his room, I know it's wrong but I couldn't help it. I wanted to touch everything in his flat and now I feel so <u>guilty</u>. I think that Aunt Meredith might like him and I don't know what to do.

I am happy you can stay. I wish you were here right now so we could talk. I got my Intermediate results and I did all right in everything. Congratulations on you passing too.

Please write soon.
    With love from crazy Sandra XOXOX

P.S. Mum just told me a lady rang about Kitty and I have
to meet her at the flat tomorrow.

As she walked the footpath to Mister L'estrange's flat, the key
a stone-weight in her pocket, Sandra's heart was heavy with misery.
She wasn't sure why she didn't want the lady to recognize Kitty. If
the kitten belonged to her, wasn't that good for Kitty? Then she
would never need to use the key again ... there would be no more
confronting thoughts about his bed, no matter how much she
desired to lie there again.

She couldn't help imagining how the next time she went
to the flat, she would slide beneath the sheet, stretch her legs
across the crisp expanse. Last night she had conjured Mister
L'estrange in her waking dreams, danced with him, wanted
to feel his hands the same tender way he'd stroked the kitten.
Stupid stupid stupid.

A small woman in baggy overalls, tee-shirt and boots waited
at the entrance to the flats. Shading her eyes against the bright
morning sun, she asked, 'Sandra?'

What funny clothes, Sandra observed with surprise ... she's
not much older than me. But she felt a pang of sorrow at the
pleasant voice, the lovely smile ... this must be the owner – she'd
be sure to have a dear little pet like Kitty. Sandra led her into the
foyer and up the stairs, turning the key in the lock for perhaps the
last time.

The kitten wasn't immediately visible as Sandra glanced around
the flat. 'She might be hiding,' she suggested. 'We'll have to hunt
for her. Sometimes she curls up on the piano stool.'

Kitty was curled on the stool as expected, regarding them with secret, half-closed eyes. Sandra stroked the little bony head. 'I called her Kitty,' she said. 'Is she yours?'

'Oh yes, thank you very much for finding her. Isn't she a dear little thing? Her name's *Mimi*. I haven't lived around here very long, and I couldn't believe it when she disappeared. Then I saw your notice. What a relief!' She rattled on, caressing the kitten which struggled to be free. 'I don't know how she escaped ... I share a house, maybe someone left a window open. I'll have to find somewhere more secure to live.'

She felt Sandra's gaze. 'I'm sorry,' she said, 'I haven't even introduced myself. 'I'm Irene. Or Rene for short.'

'I'm Sandra.'

Irene hunted around in her voluminous pockets. 'Your reward,' she pressed a pound note into Sandra's hand. 'Thank you for looking after her.' Then, surprisingly, she turned to the piano. 'What a beauty, would you mind if I take a peek?'

Sandra raised the lid, glancing sideways at the young woman, absorbing her pale reddish hair, the delicate fairness of her skin, the paint-spotted overalls, paint smears on each slim arm.

Irene sat at the piano, glanced at Sandra for a brief moment, then ran her fingers experimentally over several keys. 'I've never heard of a Feurich. Can I have a go?'

At Sandra's nod, she played a series of chords, then fiddled with a melody for a few bars. Sandra watched her fingers ripple across the keyboard, bemused by the odd thought that Irene assumed this was her home.

Irene gently closed the piano. 'I was never much good,' she said. 'Thanks for that, it was lovely to play again, but I don't really miss it I suppose, I'm too busy.'

'What are you doing?'

'I moved from Taree a month ago. I had enough of life in a country town and my brother with his horrible ferrets. And ...' she pulled a face, 'a crazy boyfriend who wanted to get married. God, the last thing on earth ... right now I'm helping a bloke paint the inside of a house. It's rather fun while I look for a job.'

Sandra scrambled for something to say. 'Me too,' she confided. 'We moved from Curradeen a year ago.'

She was about to add that she didn't really live here, that it was her piano teacher's flat, when Irene scooped up the kitten, holding her tightly. 'I better get going, thanks again,' and with a swift kiss on Sandra's cheek, she was gone. Sandra heard her boots echo down the stairs, the foyer door flump shut. The flat settled into an incredible emptiness.

Before he departed, Mister L'estrange had said, 'Keep my piano warm, play it whenever you visit Kitty, if you want to.' She'd only needed to feed the kitten by herself for one day, and the sadness was intolerable. Sandra had no idea if the small animal in Mister L'estrange's flat had been the only reason to visit, or did she wish to be there, cat or no cat? She couldn't – didn't want to – answer her own question.

Returning to the piano, her fingers swept over the first bars of *Clair de Lune* .... *andante tres expressif* ... how she loved that opening. But the concert had become a faded memory, and she shut the lid.

It was impossible not to go into his bedroom again. This time, she opened the wardrobe. Inside, a row of shirts on coat hangers, several ties and the suit he'd worn to the concert. She caught at the shirts, held them to her face, but they simply smelled of freshly laundered cotton. Taking a jacket from its hanger, she slipped her arms into the sleeves, stroked the leather with inquisitive fingers, wondered at the warmth, the lightness of it, her body feeling small inside its broad-shouldered shell. Hesitating by the desk, she gently slid open a drawer, all the time telling herself: this is an intrusion in my teacher's life, he would hate me if he knew. There'd be no more lessons and that was a thought too terrible to bear. At the front of the drawer lay a single piece of note paper, startling her with the lines:

> To Meri ~
> 'My heart, the bird of the wilderness has found its sky
> in your eyes'
>   ~ for you, by the poet Tagore.

His handwriting. So he loved her. Had Aunt Meredith read it? Why is it still in his desk? Reluctant tears filled her eyes. That's it, I'm being ridiculous, a stupid little girl with my own stupid little fantasies. Her instinct was to screw the paper up, hurl it away before he could give it to her, but just as gently as she had retrieved it, she replaced it in the drawer. I can still be with him through our music, she thought ... he's twenty seven, in four months I'll be sixteen, is it so impossible? Again, she couldn't answer.

After Sandra washed the bowls that Kitty had used and thrown out the dirty newspapers from the tray, the entire flat appeared normal once more, ready for Mister L'estrange's return. She placed the key on the mantelpiece, closed the door behind her. The room was restored, No one had been there. No one at all. Truly and utterly the *finale*.

Angela was just going out the front gate. 'Goodness me,' she said, 'you look like you've seen a ghost. What's up?'

'Nothing.' Sandra stopped at the gate. What could she possibly say, anyway? 'It was the lady's kitten. I left his key there.'

'Good girl, that's the best result for the kitten. What about coming into town with me? We haven't been shopping together for ages.'

'Maybe…' Disconsolate, Sandra shrugged one shoulder. No Mister L'estrange, no Kitty.

Disregarding Sandra's mood, Angela said, 'Go and change into a dress, we'll have lunch at Cahills, would you like that?'

'With Prue?'

'Prue's gone to the beach as usual, with her gang of girls.' Angela adjusted her hat, adding, 'Hurry up, and I'll wait for you – you can help me find your father a present.'

14th Dec. 61.

Dear Emilia,

I wrote to you yesterday but I have to tell you that I found out Mr. L is definitely in love with Auntie and I know I mustn't be jealous. I have to GROW UP!

I suppose I've been dreaming because I've missed Nick for so long. I made a mistake and thought Mr. L really cared for me, but I'm only his music student and he is encouraging me to do my best. I should be happy for Auntie because she deserves to find someone nice, and he is nice, I know I didn't think so at first.

I got your letter, I'm very happy that you can visit, I missed you so much all this year and you are my best friend forever. What date will you get here?

A nice lady called Irene came to get Kitty. She looked funny dressed in overalls all dirty with paint. I don't mind because I know Kitty has a good home. I left the key in Mr. L's flat so I can't go back even if I want to, which I don't.

Now I'm sad because everyone seems so busy with what they're doing. Magazines write about typical teenagers who get moody, cranky, self-centred etc etc. and that's me! Who writes these horrid things?

Thank goodness exams are over and school's finished. I wish you were here right now.

Love from Sandra XOXOXO

"Ferrari's Farm."
19th Dec. 61.

Dear Sandra,

I read your first letter lots of times that you wrote on the 13th. I don't know what to say because you didn't ought to go in your teacher's room and stickybeak and lie on his bed. I would like to know what it feels like to love someone, Lofty is nice and we have a good time and that, and the pictures was fun, but he's Lofty and I don't really want to kiss him like he does.

But you can't really love your music teacher because you would get in trouble if someone found out because he is your teacher, like at school do you remember when that girl left after going with our sports teacher? I hope that helps because you sound despirit. You never write about Nick, don't you love him any more?

I hope you won't be cross I talked to Mamma and she said you will grow out of this big emotion because often what comes suddenly may not last and you are only 15 and he is 12 years older. It's good that you left the key behind and you will feel better now.

My New Year's resolution is when I leave school I won't work in the shop but I will learn how to help people after accidents, like Nick. Will you make a resolution this year?

I will be there on Saturday 13th January, I have my ticket packed already in my new handbag. Cheer up!

Love from Emilia. xoxo

Tyrell St, Randwick.
23rd Dec. 61.

Dear Emilia

You will get this letter next year. Don't worry, I'll get over Mr. L, because it's like your mother said, but Nick is my first love and he will be my friend forever even if I never see him again.

I've been living in a romance novel like Mills & Boon, waiting for a tall, dark and handsome man to sweep me off my feet. Actually Mr. L is not that tall. Oh well, I always said I don't want a boyfriend, but sometimes I think it might be nice.

We decorated our house and Xmas dinner will be at our place. We're having roast turkey and Auntie made a proper Christmas pudding full of threepenny bits, 2 sixpences and a lucky shilling. She made real brandy sauce which tastes so rich I could eat a whole bowl.

You'll soon be here and I'll be at Central station to meet your train, it's going to be wonderful! Happy New Year !!! I will think of a resolution this time.

With love from Sandra XOXOX

nine.

Holiday crowds filled the city stores and Christmas carols echoed from doorways. David Jones' windows were traditionally arranged with their diligent puppets endlessly sewing and tapping tiny items. Three more days before everything closed for Christmas.

Don often pottered in the garden in the early mornings before the heat set in. Over breakfast one day he announced that the Menzies government had been re-elected by the narrowest margin of one seat. Sandra thought her father didn't look pleased as he went out the back door. For half an hour they could hear him hammering in tomato stakes. She'd heard her mother insist they were 'comfortably off' so what was the problem?

Angela and Prue went into town for last-minute gifts, leaving Sandra at home with Meredith, who arrived early to help decorate the dining room. They spent an hour at the table, snipping and gluing more red and green tissue paper chains, adding to those Prue had already made. Then Sandra held the ladder for Meredith to reach up to each corner of the picture rails with paper chains and sticky tape.

It was an ideal chance to hear about William's home-coming, otherwise it would be next year and she might never discover how the story ended. Or *if* it ever ended!

She waited until Meredith fixed the final chain. 'You haven't finished telling me about William,' she said. 'Please, while no one's around?'

Meredith pressed the last piece of sticky tape firmly onto the corner and climbed down the ladder. 'I thought I came over for the decorating – it looks pretty, doesn't it? All we need are some candles. If Angela hasn't got any, I'll bring some from home.' Then she added with a smile, 'There's really not much more to say. Let's take some cold drinks and find a shady spot in the garden. I'm so hot, it must be over ninety.'

With glasses of lemonade, they settled on the garden seat under the patchy shade of the peach tree. 'You got up to when William came home,' Sandra reminded her. 'Was he all right?'

'You're like a dog with a bone, aren't you? You'll be brilliant if you attack your music with the same energy! Ah well, yes, William eventually returned home. He was very, very sad. He escaped serious wounding but he'd got so thin. It wasn't that he couldn't talk about those years – when he was home on leave he told me about the beautiful river valleys, how in springtime the hillsides were covered in flowers… He also told me how they fought the Chinese, often in pitch dark, the ruined villages and roads choked with poor refugees. He had nightmares, awful dreams, and I couldn't do anything except hold him until the storm passed. But it never really passed – it was as if a bogeyman, a blackness had seeped into his mind.

'What sort of dreams?'

'He would never say. Yet to me, the names of some of those battles sounded like musical notes: Chonju, Maryang San, Kapyong. And I wonder what it was all for, because after the armistice it ended up divided almost the same.' Meredith ran her fingers along the garden seat, picked at a flaw with a varnished fingernail. 'I'm sorry, I honestly don't know why I told you that, it's got nothing to do with how you met Nick and I met Will.'

'It's all part of the story – Nick's accident, and how William went away – but he came back, so I don't understand—'

'All right, but remember *you asked me.* After Will left the army, he did odd jobs, anything at all. We tried to live a normal life, but he had too much time on his hands – too much time to dwell on the horrors of the war.'

'Why didn't you go back to Austinmer, have picnics?'

'Picnics! Oh, Sandra, a picnic wouldn't solve anything. The joy had gone out of his life. He tried to hide it, but I knew that under his smiles he was deeply disturbed. He was often cranky, so unlike the William I knew.'

'Were you living in your house then?'

'Yes, we were in our little home. We painted it, and made it look beautiful. He built the trellis, laid brick paving for our garden chairs…' Meredith's voice trailed off as she drank her lemonade, until Sandra feared that she wasn't going to finish before the family arrived home.

'You wanted the end of the story, dear Sandra,' Meredith said, with affection, 'and I know you'll never leave me alone if I don't tell you.' She took a deep breath and went on, 'I'm sorry, it's not a happy ending. Will didn't ever get back either his physical strength or his spirit. He took to walking the streets at night, just walking. I went with him a few times, until he asked me not to. He'd come home in the early morning, dog tired, so tired he hardly knew where to put his feet.'

Sandra pictured the dark streets of Bronte, street lights shining at intervals, the lonely figure.

'Couldn't he see a doctor, or someone who could help?'

'He could've got help, but William was stubborn … he said no one would listen because apart from his frost-bitten ears, he had no obvious injury. He quit the army and that was the end of it…

lost, roaming the streets alone. One morning he simply didn't come home.'

Alarmed, Sandra put her hand on Meredith's arm. She hadn't expected this kind of an ending. 'Did he run away?'

'No. Perhaps that would have been better. The police came to my door. They sat me down on our sofa and told me William had been hit by a tram. He died beside the tramline, and the tram went on its way without the driver, poor man, realizing what had happened.'

Sandra was aghast. She could never have imagined anything so shocking – to survive a war, and then get hit by a tram. The ache filled her throat but it was very important not to cry and somehow she managed to stifle it.

Meredith took Sandra's hand in hers. She wasn't in tears but her face looked immeasurably sad. 'You see, Sandra, Will came home in his body, but he never really came home to me.'

It was impossible to speak and Sandra sat beside her aunt, their hands together. Poor Auntie, who always looked so lovely with such a beautiful smile, but all the time hiding the sadness in her heart. Finally she asked, 'Do Mum and Dad know?'

'Donald knows about Will's accident and why I'm so financially well off, but I'm not sure that your mother knows the full story. She never met William – I suppose she might guess about the photograph. After I laid him with his family in the cemetery, it was easier for me to manage my loss by not talking about it, and then it became normal. I tried to accept it, but sometimes when I'm alone, I miss him still.'

'You always look so serene and confident.'

'Ha, my defence after I lost William. But when I found his photograph in the bottom drawer, Will's face so smiling and loving, I decided it was time to put his death behind me, to remember our happy times. And talking to you too. I had no idea it would be such a long story, but it's been good, and I hope it's been good for you, too. I wanted to show you that when we lose someone we love, however it happens, no matter how hard, somehow we must try to accept it and eventually come to terms with the change.'

Sandra squeezed her aunt's hand. 'Thank you for telling me, Auntie, I won't say anything to Mum.'

'It doesn't matter if you do, because I'm so much happier lately. Maybe it's because I've been having such a good time at the Troc with your piano teacher. Eric's taught me to dance the *bossa nova*. It's such marvellous fun.'

Dancing with Mister L'estrange, dancing again with *Eric*... Distantly she heard Meredith speaking, and dragged herself away from his bed and back to the garden seat.

Her face alight with pleasure, Meredith continued, 'He's been a tonic for me – to talk and laugh. We went to the Stadium a couple of weeks ago to see Frank Sinatra, I can't tell you how wonderful that was. All those songs, and my favourite, *In the Still of the Night*... so divine. I feel that I might possibly fall in love again. With *Eric*!' She paused. 'I can see you're surprised, but remember, that's a big *big* secret.'

'What about *him*?' Sandra couldn't say his name, the name she'd snuffled into his pillow only last week. Now she could barely speak for the load of guilt lodged in her chest. She couldn't imagine ever again being able to sit in the same room as Mister L'estrange, accidentally brush his arm as he sat beside her at the keyboard, knowing that she'd crept into his room, lain in his bed with idiotic romantic ideas and emotions, and all the time, deep down, wondering if he'd noticed anything amiss on his return.

'Oh, he knows,' Meredith almost sang. 'He knows, and he's happy too. Haven't you noticed?'

Sandra thought for an instant and the realization hit her. 'He laughs more!' she said, recalling how jovial he was with the kitten. And that poem in his desk...

'And so do I. He's so nice, Sandra, but you know that already. Before he left, we had dinner at *Beppi's,* the Italian restaurant...' Meredith laughed. 'You know, I like to think of friendship as a little boat, maybe a wooden row boat, a clinker? When love comes, it's like we've put up a sail and as that little boat zips along, we have to work to keep it sailing straight and true. I'm not sure how deep my feeling is for Eric – I'll wait and see, but whatever happens, my boat is strong now, and I won't let it sink.'

Still laughing, she said, 'This is going to be the happiest Christmas for years!' She kissed Sandra's cheek, smoothed her hair. 'Dear Sandra, I hope your story has a happy ending, that you see Nick again, and have a chance to build that beautiful friendship you've been longing for.'

From inside the house Angela's voice called, 'Hellooo!' They heard the front door bang shut behind her. 'There you both are...' She beckoned from the kitchen window, 'Sandy, I need some help to unload the shopping.'

With a wry glance at Meredith, Sandra gave her aunt's arm a final pat. 'She still calls me Sandy, when I've asked her not to, so many times,' she grizzled.

'I'll have a word to her,' Meredith offered, flinging her a smile. 'Our names are important to us. Come on, let's go and help.'

"Ferrari's Farm."
2nd. January, 62.

Dear Sandra,

I hope you had a happy Christmas and you liked my present. I thought the little angel statue could look after you. Your auntie's pudding tasted yummy, I bet.

141

For Christmas I got a swimming cozzie and a bathing cap with pink flowers, and I got rubber thongs for the beach because there's no cathead thorns like here.

Roger gave me a big box of Cadbury chocolates, you will be as surprised as me. I didn't know where to look but he knows I only like him as a friend. My brothers keep teasing me about him.

Maybe we will get to be prefects this year. Don't forget to meet me at the station or I will get lost!

with love from Emilia XXXOOO

Tyrell St., Randwick.
6th January, 1962

Dear Emilia,

I hope you had a happy Christmas. I put your pretty angel on my dressing table and every morning when I wake up it's the first thing I see. Thank you thank you!

Our turkey was delicious and Prue and I ate lots of Auntie's pudding to see who could find all the money. Mum's icing on her Christmas cake was that hard, Prue peeled hers off and put it in a box. Mum says it's called Royal Icing and Dad said he needed a hammer but he ate it anyway.

We got clothes and books for Christmas, Auntie gave me proper silk French knickers that she sewed herself. We all gave her a box of piano LP records and she gave Mum a novel called "Forever Amber." Mum said where did she buy it because it was banned until 3 years ago. I want to read that book!

Auntie brought champagne and I think she got tiddly because when she carried in the plates she danced cha cha— cha and sang and laughed lots. I drank 2 glasses in the kitchen when no one was looking and got a fizzy feeling after. I asked Dad if I could have a glass with my turkey but he said <u>No because I'm not old enough</u>. Ha ha.

It was so funny, because Auntie wanted Mum to dance and said in a fake man's voice, Annngela, come and be deliiirious with me. Mum didn't know what to do at first, but then she danced with Auntie and they looked so silly I nearly died laughing and fell off my chair!

Dad watched all the Davis Cup on TV and we beat Italy 5-0 and Rod Laver and Roy Emerson are heroes !!

I know the whole story about William now and I will tell you when I see you because it's got a very sad ending. She's happy with Mr. L so I should be glad too.

But I'm feeling really hollow inside because my life has big gaps in it and I don't know how to fill them. I will probably grow into a hermit alone in my room making up music and never going out, but at least it will be ME, and I will find out who I am and how to follow my own road. So that was my New Year's resolution.

Sorry this is a mad letter! One more week and you'll be here.

love from Sandra XOX and see you soon!

※

Any minute now the train would arrive. Sandra and her father waited on the platform, not sure exactly from which carriage Emilia would emerge. It was almost eight months since she'd visited the Ferraris, and she knew Emilia would be excited on her first visit ever, to Sydney.

'Here it comes!' Slowly, slowly the huge engine drew nearer, hissing steam with each turn of the wheels, the engine-driver guiding the train to a halt, where with a long sigh, it hissed a final gush of steam from the exhausts.

Sandra stood on tip-toe, the better to see, as all along the train, one by one, people began to step down to the platform. She stared at the crowd, searching for Emilia. And then she saw her ... dear Emilia: taller, hair cut very short into dark curls, hemline demurely well below her knees, she hurried towards them, carrying a suitcase, a handbag over one arm.

'Sandy, Sandy,' Emilia threw her arms around Sandra, kissing her on each cheek. 'I had such a lovely trip. Hello Mr Abbott. Gee, thanks,' she said as Don took her case. 'It was so exciting to go on a big train all by myself but it's too wobbly in the toilets. I liked the buffet car best where you buy lunch or icecream and sit at a table ... I only bought a cup of tea 'cause Mamma packed my sandwiches.'

Without pause for breath as they left the station, Emilia burbled on, 'There's so many people here, are we in the middle of Sydney? Mamma sends her love and Pa said *buongiorno*, as he wouldn't send his love, because he's a man and men don't say that. Nonna too, she sends you *un bacio grande*, that's a great big kiss. Ooh, look at that huge clock up there ...'

They reached the street as close by, evening church bells rang. Entranced, Emilia stopped to listen, tilting her head to one side. 'That's so pretty,' she said, eyes sparkling with pleasure. Now she was quite out of puff and walked quietly beside Sandra as Don steered them towards his car.

'Sandra's been looking forward to your arrival,' he told Emilia. 'All we've heard lately has been: when Emilia gets here, can we go here, there and everywhere.' He smiled, 'First off, home we go. And tomorrow, we're all going to Taronga Zoo.'

Sandra showed Emilia into her bedroom, where she'd made a big effort to create some space by putting all her clothes away in wardrobe and drawers. 'You're sharing with me; we can fit into my bed, don't you think?'

'We'll fit,' Emilia admitted with a giggle, 'you're fatter and I'm thinner, so we'll balance each other.'

'We'll be awake half the night 'cause we've got so much to talk about. You have to tell me all about Lofty and Roger and everything that's happened in Curradeen.' Regretfully she added, 'And Nick, if you ever see him.' Looking into Emilia's eyes, she knew Emmy wanted to ask about her piano teacher, but he must stay locked away.

They stood side-by-side in front of the mirror – Sandra's tell-all mirror – regarding their changed selves. Emilia hitched up her skirt, looked critically at her knees.

'I want to pin my hem up shorter – I can let it down again before I go home or I'd get in trouble.'

'Mum will help, she won't mind,' Sandra suggested. 'I like your hair, it looks like Gina Lollobrigida's. Remember *Trapeze*? I *loved* that film.'

'I don't get called a fat dago anymore, and some boys whistle at me. Mamma says take no notice, but I often sneak a look. The motor bike gang still hangs about town. One of them is dreamy-looking.'

'I bet your mother doesn't know that's what you think. I remember one of them looked like James Dean in his black leather jacket and jeans, the way he used to slouch.'

Emilia opened her suitcase, kneeling to sort through folded clothes. 'I've got something for you,' she said mysteriously.'

The small parcel was wrapped in shiny red paper, tied with a ribbon. With great curiosity, Sandra unwrapped it, peeled open the silver foil inside, to find a large chunk of what might be cake, an aroma of citrus and dried fruit.

'Nonna's *panettone*… Christmas bread that we eat at breakfast,' Emilia explained. 'Nonna wanted to share it with you.'

'Mmm, it smells delicious, we can have it tomorrow. She's very kind, your granny.'

'I've got something else for you but maybe you should wait till after dinner?'

'Nooo, I don't want to wait. What is it?'

'I can't exactly say,' Emilia produced an envelope. 'Now or later?'

'A letter? Who'd be writing to me, is it from Lofty?'

Emilia giggled and shook her head. Hiding the envelope behind her back, her face wore a mischievous grin. 'Which hand will you have?'

'Don't be a tease, you're the only one who writes to me. Okay... your left hand.'

Emilia put out her empty left hand, but before Sandra could say anything, in her other hand she produced the envelope.

Sandra gleefully snatched at the plain white business envelope. On the front was printed in ink: Sandra, a curlicue drawn beneath it. She sat on her bed and Emilia came to sit beside her. She wondered if it could be something to do with Curradeen high school, or perhaps a letter from Miss Brooks? No, Miss Brooks would probably write on mauve paper, and the school would type her name – anyway, why would the school be writing to her? Curiouser and curiouser.

The flap was barely stuck down and she flipped it open, revealing a single page. She caught her breath... surely not, after all this time...

"Wilga Park,"
Denalbo Rd., Curradeen.
11 Jan 62.

Dear Sandra,

Here is a picture of Honey for you to see how beautifully she's growing. She follows Toffee like a good little filly should, & suddenly she'll go for a mad run across the paddock, kicking up her heels. She's great fun to watch.

My father has given me the green light to study architecture this year, Mum must have got in his ear that I'll never make a sheep farmer. I'll be in Sydney for a few days next month to enrol & organize living at the college then back home until uni begins.

I've chucked away my sticks, but only so-so on horseback. Friends will look after Toffee & Honey when I leave.

I'll let you know when I'm down & maybe we can meet in that teapot coffee shop if you'd like to?

It's going to be a cracker year!

Yours sincerely,
Nick

As she read this solid evidence of Nick's wish for friendship, Sandra was speechless, and tears of unexpected emotion seeped from her eyes. If only he knew how she'd longed for something like this, some proof that he might care. With shaking fingers, she gave the letter to Emilia.

A glossy photograph slipped from the envelope onto her lap: picture of a young horse, the chestnut foal stood quietly beside Toffee as she nuzzled the mare's flank. 'Ooh, she's so sweet,' Sandra cried. 'Look at her little tail, it's like a brush.'

Emilia put the letter back in its envelope. 'Gee, I had no idea. When Nick came in the shop for an order the other day, I told him I'm going to visit you, and yesterday he turned up with the letter.' She put her arm around Sandra's shoulders. 'I know you've been so mixed up,' she said. 'Put the letter under your pillow tonight, it'll help you find out what you truly feel.'

Sandra already knew how she felt – she didn't need Nick's letter beneath her pillow to invoke his presence. For months her dreams had been empty of the tall young man who'd waited for her on the Town Hall steps. He no longer stood beside her as she played the piano; she hadn't heard his voice, his laugh, his affectionate name for her. It seemed almost impossible that she had banished him like that, without even noticing he'd gone.

But with the comfort of Nick's friendly letter, the fantasies which had recently dominated her thoughts retreated like ghosts. Emilia had innocently brought with her the echoes of her old life – that old life with all its promises and possibilities.

To celebrate Emilia's arrival, Sandra created a centrepiece for the dinner table with Christmas candles and flowers from the garden. Angela cooked Pork Hawaiian, and a dessert of cherry flummery with whipped cream served in her special pink glass bowls.

'It's delicious, Mrs Abbot,' Emilia said, 'but I can't eat any more 'cause I'm stuffed full.'

Everyone laughed and Sandra peeked sideways to see her mother's reaction, mindful that it was the first time Emilia had ever eaten a meal with them. To Angela, Emilia seemed much improved, but she couldn't help smiling at the familiar, careless speech, and made a mental note to be sure neither of her daughters used the same expression. Goodness me, *Stuffed!*

By nine o'clock, Prue had disappeared to her bedroom. Only the lounge room light still burned. Sandra and Emilia sat alone on the garden seat beneath the peach tree while high in the sky a half moon sailed in drifts of cloud. Heads close together, they talked and giggled, until tired of slapping at mosquitoes, they went to bed, to continue in whispers with all that needed to be told.

In their shared bed, Emilia's curly head rested on the pillows, her arm flung out from the covering sheet on this warm night, her sleeping breath a gentle purr. As a breeze stirred through the garden, the wooden venetians knocked a soft *tok tok* against the window sill. Emilia, here at last – so tranquil in her sleep – eyelids heavy, cheek turned aside.

Beside her, Sandra lay deep in a maze of thoughts. She breathed in for the count of three, trying to unscramble their chatter: so many changes: about school, the kitten, the marching girls that never were, Lofty... Nick's letter.

Mentally she hummed a few bars of Kitty's favourite *Cradle Song*... if she could concentrate on that one line for a moment... Prue had badly wanted to keep the kitten – would it have mattered to their old ginger cat? Might Mister L'estrange have kept Kitty if he hadn't been going away? What was I playing at? she pondered – fooling myself with wild imaginings of Mister L'estrange. But when I open a new piece of music will he be there? Is he somewhere in my songs, like Nick used to be? She carefully turned over so she could glimpse the sky through the slats of the blind.

How would she know if she'd chosen the right road? Still within the echo of Mister L'estrange's encouragement to compose music, it seemed perfect. Again she heard those six hypnotic notes from the bassoon, remembrance of Stravinsky's *Berceuse*. Floating, sublime.

Breathing quietly, colours slipping unbidden onto her mind's palette, she could think about this evening – Emilia saying, 'I have something for you.' Gosh, what a surprise. Emmy couldn't possibly know that simply by bringing me Nick's letter she's helped me turn a page, and now I'm free to compose *Winter's Day*. And I'll make up a song for Emmy too, because I love her as my dearest friend, and my song without words will be for her.

Sleep was nudging her, and she imagined Aunt Meredith's voice saying, 'The best is yet to come.' She felt with careful fingers for the envelope beneath her pillow ... it was still there. Sinking past the edge of sleep into a dream, she whispered the words ...

4

Emilia laughed to see herself in the mirror as they packed up beach towels and bathing caps, and pulled on their swimmers. Her skin was very brown except where she had worn long shorts, shirt and socks to work on the farm.

'—From working in our vegie garden,' she complained. 'Pa says I've got a farmer's suntan.'

Sandra laughed with her, slathering coconut oil on Emilia's white back. It was her dear, sweet Emmy, never giving any hint of being bothered if things weren't right – a beautiful, grown-up Emmy.

The sand was pocked with yesterday's footprints, but this early in the morning, there were few people at the beach.

Sandra could hardly keep up with her as Emilia ran up and down – now splashing into the water, now dashing along the high tide mark – sometimes pouncing on a shell, then running back to show Sandra. Every so often she stopped to gaze at the ocean, arms held out wide as if to encompass the horizon.

Out of breath, they slowed to a walk. 'I want to see those mermaids,' Emilia said. 'Where are they?'

Sandra pointed. 'There, sitting on that great big rock below the cliff.'

It was a race towards the northern end of the beach. As they ran, a wave broke over the rock, sending streamers of white foam cascading like a waterfall over both rock and mermaids where they sat, tails gracefully curled. One mermaid held a hand as if to shade her eyes as she gazed across the ocean.

'Gee, they must've posed in the nuddy.' Emilia giggled. 'That one looks like she's scratching her back.' Imitating the mermaid, she stuck out her chest, one arm raised. 'How did they put them up there, 'cause they must be real heavy?'

Sandra self-consciously copied Emilia's pose. 'It's fake bronze. They're supposed to be modelled on Miss Australia Surf.'

'Can we get closer?'

'Nuh-uh, the waves are too high. The tide's got to be very low so you can walk out on the flat rocks.

'Oh too bad,' Emilia said. 'Anyway, let's go for a swim, I want to show you how good I've got.'

The beach was becoming crowded: families lolled on blankets spread beneath umbrellas, sunbakers lay glistening with oil. Pulling on her flowery bathing cap, Emilia ran into the water, dodging among children building sandcastles and paddling in the shallows near their mothers.

Maybe today, Sandra decided, she would plunge in beside her, knowing Emmy was now a strong swimmer to keep her company. Of course there were no sharks ... She gritted her teeth and followed, calling, 'Don't go out so far!'

Emilia waited, bobbing in the surf. Sandra was satisfied she could still stand, and regardless of the occasional wallop from a larger wave, she was determined to go deeper – to not be a sook today.

Several boys floated nearby, splashing each other. One swept his hand fast across the water, sending a spray towards Emilia, who shrieked and splashed back at him. It started a frenzied splashing and ducking among the boys, with occasional splashes at Emilia, who continued to play, bobbing up and down, almost losing the top of her costume from a loose strap until Sandra grabbed her arm.

'Fix your cozzie,' she scolded, knowing she sounded like her mother. 'They can nearly see your—'

Cutting her off with a cheeky smile, Emilia dived deep into the waves. When she popped up, her costume was firmly tied in place.

'You're mad,' Sandra told her. 'You shouldn't do things like that.'

'Oh, boo hoo, things like what?' Emilia laughed. 'I'm just having fun.'

Back at the flags where they'd left their towels, Sandra applied more zinc to her nose and lips, but Emilia refused. 'I'm not putting that white stuff on my face,' she said. 'I won't burn, I never do.'

The boy who had first splashed Emilia sat nearby with his friends. Emilia kept looking over her shoulder in his direction, until finally their stares coincided, and with a big smile, she took her towel and went to sit with him.

Content to stay by herself, Sandra wondered how some girls got to flirt so easily. Meredith flirted with waiters, and now it was Emilia, flirting like mad with these boys. Maybe, Sandra thought, she took too much notice of dire warnings from her mother about 'encouraging the wrong type,' as Angela put it. 'Nice girls don't behave like that.' Like what?

It had been so easy to be friends with Nick. Sandra wasn't interested in the boys that Emilia was talking to, and maintained a steady watch on the surfers. The southerly breeze had strengthened, blowing sand and tossing umbrellas.

Emilia draped her towel around her shoulders, and after the boys returned to swim, she teased Sandra, saying, 'They're nice boys, and they're on holidays too. Why didn't you come and say hello?'

Sandra shrugged, relieved to see Meredith waving to them from the esplanade.

A glistening glass-topped counter filled with trays of biscuits drew them into the café. *'Buongiorno, buongiorno, signorinas,'* the patron of the café welcomed them.

Meredith chose a table, while Sandra and Emilia surveyed the array of pastries, *macarons* and *biscotti* under the glass counter.

'Ooh,' Emilia sighed. 'I wish my nonna could see this. She's such a good cook, she should open a shop in Curradeen. She makes the *best* biscuits. Wait till I tell her!'

A waiter hovered until Meredith ordered, and a plate of several different biscuits and *cannoli* was soon set on their table, alongside their cappuccinos.

Emilia took a bite from a custard-filled pastry. 'I will be fat again,' she groaned, 'and I did like being thinner.'

'Emilia, you look lovely,' Meredith said. 'Those young men can't help gazing at you two girls, so pretty in your sundresses.'

Sandra sneaked a look from the corner of her eye at the several men lounging on their Vespas at the kerb; wide-eyed, Emilia stared straight back at them until Sandra gave her a poke, saying, 'You're not supposed to notice.'

'Why didn't Prue want to come?' Meredith asked. 'And your mother ... I thought she'd enjoy an outing with us?'

'Mum only likes the cafeteria at David Jones,' Sandra licked the last of her custard from a finger. 'Or Cahills Restaurants.'

'And Prue?'

'Oh, she goes nearly every day to her girlfriend's house.'

Meredith nodded, signalling to the waiter. 'Shall we order a *gelato* now?'

'Yes please, Auntie. I'm going to have strawberry. What'll you have, Em?'

Emilia had finished her cappuccino and was spooning the remaining froth from around her cup, occasionally casting sidelong glances at the young men.

'Pistachio, *per favore*,' she said to the waiter, rolling her r's with an impish smile.

y

Their days were filled with talk and laughter – giggles in bed at night until a sleepy voice called from down the hallway, 'Sssh, you two.'

Angela was surprised at how voluble Emilia had become. She was no longer the shy, inarticulate girl that she remembered from Curradeen. Don looked on with amusement, finding that Emilia brought a lightness to their home that lately had been missing.

The letter to Nick waited to be written. Sandra yearned to be alone, yet at the same time she was desperate for Emilia to stay.

Time was trickling away, busy with the remaining excursions: a ride on the great South Steyne ferry to Manly, and more icecream and *gelati* with Aunt Meredith at their favourite *pasticceria*, where Sandra bought a box of fancy biscuits for Emilia's granny.

Together they visited Rowe Street to gaze in the windows, and in Farmers department store, Emilia chose presents for all her family. On the last day, Sandra walked with Emilia to Mister L'estrange's street, to show her where she'd found the kitten, perhaps even to briefly stand in the street beneath the windows of his flat.

At an intersection, by a small miracle, she saw a girlish figure in baggy overalls about to cross the road – a figure that halted mid-step and waved to them.

Paint smears on her arms, her pale red hair tied in a bunch, Irene looked much the same as when she'd come for the kitten.

She clasped Sandra's hands in hers. 'How lucky to meet you again … how are you? You can see I'm still painting houses …' Breathless as ever, she went on: 'I wanted to let you know I found a house to share, where Mimi will be safe. Come and visit us one day. Or can I visit you, and play that beautiful piano?'

Sandra pocketed Irene's phone number. It was too complicated to explain about the old Feurich. Let it keep its secrets.

❡

Emilia had accumulated another bag full of shopping, and with her suitcase, handbag, new tote bag, and a sunhat jammed over her curls, Don shepherded her along the platform. The train for Curradeen would depart in fifteen minutes and they hurried to find her carriage, Prue running ahead to check the numbers.

'Thank you, thank you. Gee, I've had a marvellous time,' Emilia said, kissing first Don, then Angela and Prue. She folded Sandra into her arms, squeezed her tightly in a hug. 'It was real special.' Her eyes brimmed with tears. 'Write to me soon, tell me everything, about Nick, and that?'

'I promise I'll write,' Sandra said. 'And we promised not to cry, remember?'

The guard unfurled his white flag. Any minute now he would blow his whistle and wave his flag for the train to depart. Emilia leaned from her window, blowing kisses, tears running down her cheeks, her sun-burned nose. Slowly the wheels turned, steam

155

choof-choofing from the engine exhausts, until their cries of goodbye were lost to the empty steel tracks.

It was a silent drive back home. Prue hadn't wanted to come to the station and as soon as possible, she left to visit her friends. The house seemed very quiet without Emilia. Sandra's bedroom floor was strewn with items of clothing, and she stuffed some things away, closed drawers and cupboards, not wanting to tidy her room – wanting to keep Emilia just a little while longer. Under her bed lay a single stocking – from the pair Sandra had given Emilia for Christmas. She rolled it, tucking it into her drawer.

The train would hardly have got as far as Parramatta station before Sandra had torn a sheet of Bond note paper from her mother's writing pad.

ten.

The sound of piano music filled Meredith's street. It was coming from her house – all open windows – very loud, as if someone banged hard on all the keys, a foot on the pedal sustaining notes in an angry blur.

Sandra hesitated at the gate. Should she go in? They hadn't arranged to meet this morning, but it was a Saturday – not unusual for Sandra to get the bus almost to the corner and walk to Meredith's door. Now Emilia had gone home, she was keen to tell Aunt Meredith about Nick's letter.

Reluctant to knock, she waited on the step. The pianist kept playing, but quieter now, fading into a piece that Sandra recognized – she'd heard the record months ago, the same wintry day Meredith told her how she ran away with William. The music continued: precisely spaced notes, crisply controlled. Played too fast. Aunt Meredith?

She waited until the piece finished, then tentatively knocked, listened as footsteps padded to the door. Sandra's smile vanished as she looked at her aunt, always so beautifully dressed, so immaculate, but today…

'Come in, come in …' An impatient aunt, already turning away.

'It's all right, Auntie, if you're busy—'

Meredith shushed her. 'You heard the piano and you're here now, so don't worry about it. I'll put on the kettle.'

Sandra had never seen Meredith's hair like this: hanging loosely under a woollen beanie, it curled in an untidy tangle down her back. Over trousers which she'd cut off at the knees, she wore a man's shirt. This wasn't Sandra's Aunt Meredith, this was a strange Meredith – heavy-eyed, unsmiling. Even when she'd related William's death, she didn't look like this.

In the shady courtyard, beneath faded roses, Meredith spread her tray with mugs and teapot.

'I've never heard you play like that …' Sandra took up her mug, blew on the hot tea. 'Is something wrong?'

'I suppose you might as well know what's happened,' Meredith grimaced.

She got up from the table and went inside. For several minutes, Sandra sat by herself. She had grown used to waiting for Aunt Meredith, after the long, long story about William so gradually revealed over several months.

Meredith put a piece of paper on the table. Yellow-coloured, it looked official.

'Read it if you like.' Meredith drank her tea, as if now she ignored the telegram.

Below a royal crown at the top, the message was printed in block letters:

**FAMILY ILLNESS DOUBT RETURN SORRY WILL WRITE
ERIC**

'I know telegrams are expensive, and he's in England,' Meredith said. 'But no "Dear Meredith." No "love Eric" like any *normal* person would write.' She sounded angry again, like the music Sandra heard from the street.

'He says he'll write—'

Meredith brushed it aside. 'It's as if there was nothing between us, as if he doesn't care.'

'Golly, Auntie, after what you told me, I'm sure he cares.' If only she could tell her aunt about the precious words on that slip of paper in Mister L'estrange's desk…

'You could talk to Dad or Mum—'

'Are you joking? You only know about Eric because you're his pupil. If we hadn't run into him at the café, I wouldn't have told you.'

'You told me about William—'

'That was different,' Meredith snapped, 'because of you and Nick.'

Nick's letter… it would have to wait. 'He hasn't told Mum he's not coming back,' she said. The fact of Mister L'estrange staying on in England, for however long, gave her a strangely sad little ache in her chest. There was nothing she could say.

Meredith snatched up the telegram and stowed it somewhere in the kitchen. Sandra wondered if maybe she would even throw it out. She'd never seen her aunt like this, and knew she was terribly hurt. Aunt Meredith had been so happy to describe friendship as being like a little wooden boat, and how her own boat would be unsinkable.

'I'm sorry,' Meredith gave a weak smile. She pulled off the beanie, rubbing a knuckle over her sweaty forehead. 'It's William's – army issue for the Korean winter.' She stroked the thick khaki knit, fingered a ragged edge. 'I used to wear it to bed.'

Speechless, Sandra could only nod.

'I've had a horrid morning,' Meredith went on. 'I'm glad you've come, before I persecute the neighbours any more with the piano.'

'What was the piece you were playing… the loud one?'

'Oh, nothing. I was just thumping the keyboard. I had a few lessons with Eric—'

She waved her hand to fend off any response. 'No, don't say anything. I asked him if he could help me get back some of my technical skill. I didn't really meet him for the first time at the Trocadero. I suppose I wanted something to be private, as lately you seemed to be finding out about my whole life.' She gave a rueful laugh. 'All my fault.'

Sandra pondered this revelation of further secrets, while Meredith poured more tea. It was too hot, and she felt sweat prickle under her arms.

'You're a good listener. And I genuinely thought it would be good for you to hear my William story. You're right, if I'd told Donald, maybe I wouldn't have been glooming around, alone in my house for years. I never told my friends, because I thought they wouldn't understand. I was probably wrong about that, too.'

Meredith concentrated on her mug of tea, and it seemed she had nothing more to say. In the silence, words rose unbidden to Sandra's lips, as if they'd been waiting to spring out.

'Nick wrote me a letter—'

Immediately Meredith brightened. She ran her fingers through her unruly hair, twisting it into a loose knot on her neck. Leaning forward, she took Sandra's hand. 'Tell me about it? I hope it's nice news. I could do with hearing something cheerful.'

'His father said he can go to university and study architecture, like Nick always wanted. He'll be coming to enrol soon. Oh Auntie, it made me so happy to read it, and he sent a photo of his new little foal.'

'Aah,' Meredith sighed at length. 'Something good often follows something bad.'

'That's what Mister L'estrange said—' Sandra bit her tongue on it.

'Never mind, finish what you're saying. We can't censor our conversations, can we?'

'After the concert, we went to Circular Quay and he talked about good and evil in *The Firebird* and in the world. He said, Goodness eventually wins, as it should.'

'Hmpf, that's a basic truth, even if it doesn't always work out that way.'

The teapot was empty and they cleared the mugs. 'I'm going to tidy myself. Play me that lovely tango? I haven't heard it since you were here last year.'

A mess of sheet music covered the top of the piano, and more papers lay scattered on the couch as if a whirlwind had swept through the room. Sandra moved some sheets and sat at the keyboard.

'We'll go to Double Bay,' Meredith called from the bedroom. 'We haven't been there for ages. Okay?'

To answer, Sandra swept into the Albeniz *Tango* that she'd first played at the Curradeen concert … the delicate little grace notes … not too much pedal – something to make Aunt Meredith happy.

'*Olé!*' Swishing her skirt and clicking her fingers, Meredith sashayed into the room. Sandra glanced up from the keyboard. Her aunt's eyes were bright, but she couldn't tell if it was pleasure or tears.

'*Sí*, the divine tango.' Meredith gathered up tote bag and sunglasses, slipped her feet into heels. '*Viva España!* Let's go …'

7

Why was it so difficult to write to Nick! Ever since Emilia's departure, Sandra had covered scrap paper with various sentences, screwing up each one to toss in the bin. She had written so many imaginary letters when she first left Curradeen that now her brain was empty.

Dear Nick, Thank you for your letter and the photo of Honey, she looks a dear little... no, I can't write that... *she looks just like her mother and I hope you will soon ride Toffee again... here is my telephone number...* She knew her words were dry as straw and flung the ball of paper onto the floor.

Damn, bloody, blast,' she muttered, using up her store of bad words. If only she could bring back the intensity of her feelings, she was sure the words would roll off her pen by themselves. If she could write, *Dear Nick, I've missed you terribly, I know I wasn't your girlfriend...* but too much emotion had been laid bare in-between.

Nick would be coming to enrol at university in February – surely he would look up the Abbott's number in the phone book and ring her? Once again she pictured how they would meet at the coffee shop in Rowe Street – but there wasn't a single page of *Winter's Day* to give him.

Emilia had not written, except to send a thankyou card addressed to Mr and Mrs Abbott, with love to Sandra and Prue. It left a hole in her heart and every day she opened the letterbox, hoping for her own 'Miss Sandra Abbott' envelope. Impossible to compose the song for Emilia – she simply couldn't conjure up any allegro or vivace phrases.

Over a paper parcel of fish and chips at Bronte beach, Aunt Meredith acted like her normal self, although Sandra was beginning to wonder what that might be. Meredith had fibbed about meeting Mister L'estrange at the Trocadero. What else might she be fibbing about? William had been so unhappy that he walked the city streets at night – perhaps Auntie was doing that too?

Australia Day passed. The holidays were almost over. She joined Carol and her friends at the beach, enjoying the froth and slap of the waves, careful not to venture past her waist, while out in the surf, Carol yelled and splashed for her to come deeper. Where was Emilia? Be brave, her head told her, but her heart refused.

In bed, she read *Lolita* by torchlight under the sheet. Carol had lent her the novel, told her to hide it from fussy parents. But widowed Humbert's longing for young Lolita, all 'rose and honey' had too many words. Tired of the endless story, the looming threat, unwilling to know how it finished, Sandra hid the book in her wardrobe.

No piano teacher, and still no word to Angela about his return. She vowed that this year she would find another teacher, and when his family's illness had passed and he came back to Sydney, too bad... she would be gone.

And Aunt Meredith? Now Mister L'estrange emerged as a thoughtless presence that blighted their lives. Perfectly correct to send a telegram, but why hadn't he sent the promised letter to explain, to wish her 'love from Eric'. His bird of the wilderness meant nothing.

¶

Two weeks into the first term of school: a warm, still night. Prue was singing *'Bye, Bye Baby Goodbye'* over the clatter of washing up after dinner. Don sat in his usual spot on the garden seat, while Angela wandered with the hose, spraying water around her new vegetable seedlings.

Sandra pleaded to visit Aunt Meredith, and after a brief protest that her aunt would not be expecting her, Angela relented. Too hot to argue – it was a Friday night, what did it matter – Meredith had a free will, she could say if it didn't suit and send Sandra home. The bus trip was only ten minutes with a short walk at each end.

Stepping off the bus, she walked the familiar way past brick walls, privet hedges, fences looped with vines. Where front doors stood open in the heat, a murmur of voices drifted to her across front porches and gardens. From behind a fence, a circling hose sent its spray in a high arc, catching Sandra with a welcome spatter.

Light-hearted, she skipped aside, wiping her face with a handkerchief. Maybe, she thought… maybe I *will* go with Prue to the Stadium to see one of her stupid shows. It can't hurt to have a look.

A squall of starlings wheeled against the pale sky before vanishing into the depths of a camphor laurel.

Not far to go…

At the top of Aunt Meredith's street, already Sandra could hear the piano. It was not the furious banging keys from days ago. Whatever it was, Sandra had never heard these complex notes before. Her steps slowed as she neared the gate. The front door was wide open. She was about to cooee when she heard voices above the music.

Leaving her sandals at the door, Sandra soft-footed down the hallway and peeked into the lounge room. To her amazement, she saw Mister L'estrange: seated snug against Meredith on the narrow piano seat, broad-shouldered in his summer shirt, his head inclined towards Meredith's as they played a duet, both of them laughing when their hands bumped on tricky passages.

In the dimness of the hall, unsure if she should leave or stay, Sandra continued to listen – loving the lightness of Meredith's treble on the repeated phrases, the haunting, almost regretful beauty of the piece; their combined amusement.

As if she sensed Sandra waiting in the hallway, Meredith suddenly twisted around on the seat, her face flushed, still filled with music.

Mister L'estrange lifted his hands from the keyboard, pushed the errant strand of hair from his forehead. 'Aha, Sandra, you're here. So, do you like our playing?' He couldn't help his laughter. 'Poor little *Schwammerl*... Schubert composed it for his unrequited love.' Turning to Meredith, he took her hand in his and pressed it to his lips, kissed her cheek.

Catching Sandra's glance at the suitcase beside the couch, 'Straight from the airport,' he said.

Straight from the airport... She surveyed the room: empty plates and wine glasses littered the table, empty bottles, coffee cups. His coat tossed across a chair, one shoe lying as if abandoned.

By the expression on their faces as they stood beside the piano, arms around each other, Sandra recognized the depth of emotion in their embrace; knew this relationship between her aunt and Mister L'estrange was serious. And watching, she sensed Meredith's little boat would sail confidently on the wide, deep ocean. Unsinkable.

Beneath heavy clouds, drops of rain spotted the footpath. Lit by street lights, Sandra dawdled from the bus stop towards home, memory of the music blending with Aunt Meredith's happiness. With Mister L'estrange... *Eric.* Quite recovered from the surprise, a silent giggle shook her. *Uncle Eric?* I can't call him *that.*

I'll write my letter tonight, she thought, hurrying as the rain became heavier. I know the words will come easily now. *Dear Nick*...

Her footsteps beat time to a gathering rhythm in her head. Rain dampened her hair but it didn't matter. She felt exhilarated, gleeful, laughing to herself: I can hear my song!

She hummed ephemeral notes and searching for keys, found C major. A developing melody sang with the rhythmic bass notes – she saw sparkles of sunshine on frosty grass, heard the staccato hoof beats.

At the front gate, she sang the theme twice more to inscribe it on her mind. I'll write it down quickly, she decided, before I begin Nick's letter.

As Sandra turned her key in the lock, Angela met her at the door. 'I've just hung up the phone,' she said. 'Nick Morgan rang to speak to you. He'll be in Sydney tomorrow.' Her smile widened. 'He's driving down, so I gave him our address. He's going to stay for dinner.'

Sandra threw off the hot sheet on her bed and lay listening to the gentle bump of her venetian blind against the sill. No moonlight – no shadows in the rain-damp garden.

A silhouette from the lighted hall filled the doorway. 'You were gone for quite a while,' Angela said.

'Was I?' It was ages since her mother had sat on her bed for a chat. 'Auntie was playing the piano, so I stayed.'

'Is that all?'

Should she tell? The name slipped out: 'Mister L'estrange was there—'

'Goodness, so he's finally back. He's left it rather late. Whatever was he doing at Meredith's?'

'Muuum,' Sandra pleaded. 'You should've seen them playing the piano together. They looked so happy.' She certainly wasn't going to mention the suitcase.

166

'Meredith's very secretive,' Angela remarked. 'I suppose I'll eventually hear all about it.' With a flick of the sheet, she covered Sandra up, tucking it around her. 'In the morning we'll talk about your music – you've hardly played a note these holidays. Good night, sleep tight.'

As soon as she'd gone, Sandra threw off the sheet. Tomorrow, Nick's ute would turn the corner into her street. He would park out the front of their house, being careful not to scrape a wheel on the kerb. He would walk up the path, felt hat tipped to one side; knock on her door.

Long ago he'd called her 'my pretty piano player' ... unbidden, the old dream of Nick returned, and she allowed the dream to flow as easily as the first notes of her new composition. Maybe this time, she pondered, maybe not ... but one day, when we go back to that coffee shop, I'll take *Winter's Day* out of my handbag and say to Nick, 'I wrote this for you,' and give him the score, decorated with the most beautiful filigreed title that I can possibly draw. He'll be so surprised, he'll be so impressed that I composed a piece especially for him.

Then later, over their coffee cups, Nick would describe his own dream, the dream he'd confided to her that cold night over a year ago when Mrs Morgan invited everyone back to Wilga Park.

'I want to design houses,' he'd told her. 'I want to build beautiful homes for people, integral parts of their lives. Everything in harmony.' And as she listened, she'd felt his passion to create, an excitement that mirrored her original, childish ambition to be a famous pianist – her new, stronger desire to compose music.

Her pictures blurred with sleep ... whatever happens, she dreamed, I know we can be friends – two stars circling each other, drawn together but separate. That's how it will be.

No sound broke the stillness in the house except for the peaceful *tok tok* of the blind.

Perhaps, she whispered, curling her arm around the pillow, there is another little bird in the wilderness, and if I give it a chance, if I give it freedom … it will find its sky.

Notes

Edward Elgar: *Dream Children, Op.43. No.1*
Wolfgang Amadeus Mozart: *Sonata in C major, K 279 No.1*
John Field: *Nocturne No.5 in B flat major*
Johann Sebastian Bach: *French Suite No.1 in D minor, BWV812, Sarabande*
Isaac Albeniz: *Tango (Suite España) Op.165 No.2*
Franz Schubert: *Cradle Song*
Franz Schubert: *Fantasie in F minor, Op.103 D 940, Part 01* (4 hands)

Rowe Street: most of the precinct including the Hotel Australia was demolished in the early 1970s to make way for the MLC Centre.
Toujours Fidèle: French perfume by D'Orsay (translation: Always Faithful)
The Birds of the Wilderness, from *The Gardener,* Rabindranath Tagore (1861-1941), London, Macmillan and Co. Ltd, 1931.
Schwammerl (Ger.) mushroom: Franz Schubert's nickname by his close friends

The author thanks Cameron Forbes for his generous advice on references to the Korean War. Read his absorbing book: *The Korean War: Australia in the Giants' Playground*, Cameron Forbes. Pan Macmillan, 2010.

The third book
in *The Midnight Pianist* series
is coming soon:

SONG FOR EMILIA